The Lady in the Ladybug

Sharona Black

The Lady in the Ladybug

ISBN 978-1508678786

Thanks to my Facebook friends who
liked the page promoting this book,
and Long Term Care in Smith Center
for letting me read the book to the residents.
Thanks to Barbara Kuiken for lending me
a chicken doll for a fair booth dedicated to this book.
Thanks to the organizers of
The Chicken Festival where I premiered this book.

Cover art by Jeremy Martinson
Gorham, Kansas

The Lady in the Ladybug

This is a work of fiction. The story was born when I tried to write a short story about a 'wrong turn.' When that movie was popular, publishers wanted southern weird. I wrote the first couple pages, and then set it aside. But I couldn't get the three characters out of my mind. I knew I had something going, but just not sure of what. Then a lady who I had met many years ago popped into my head. She was a country woman, lived a simple life, but was interesting.

I remembered a scene from a movie, after some searching, I realized it was *The Egg and I* by Betty MacDonald, and found a copy of the movie. The scene I hoped to see was about a huge chicken.

Then the plot had to be found. What would Sugar do? Why the name Sugar? Martin? Roxy? They just sounded right. Not to be picking on anyone, just liked those names.

But what was there at stake for Sugar? Would she just grow her large produce and sell it?

A conglomeration of ideas melded in my head, and I searched for a scientific reason for each.

So the world of *The Lady in the Ladybug* was created.

This is a self-published book. All errors are my own. I had two unknown publishers interested in it, but I passed on them.

'Sharona' Sharon Black

The Lady in the Ladybug

The Lady in the Ladybug

The Explosion
Hundreds
Welcome to the Farm
Reva
Malvin, Dix, and Jo, USDA agents
Cleopatra and Chicken Soup
Bobby Click
Store Number One
Sugar Martin's Second Organic Food Store
Three and Little, Inc.
Giant Chicken
"There's Trouble in the Watermelon."
Lonny and Bolynne
That someone else goes to Glassburgh
Farina at the Farm
The TV show
Sugar the Hometown Wrestler
Rivalry
Strange Trees
Grow Big Sell Big
Globes of Light
Destruction
Strange Trees, continued
The Shining Cloth
The Tree Festival
Hugh Comes Home
Healing
Halloween
Magic Show
Will You Marry Me?
End of the Season
One Year Later

The Lady in the Ladybug

The Lady in the Ladybug

The Explosion

Sod Roxalena told of a booming flash of light. One summer evening about dusk, lavender smoke swirled out of a cloudburst, and stones covered the ground like hail. For an hour, the thickest of it delivered onto the Roxalena farm.

In autumn and early winter of that year, a scare came upon the family. Globes of light. A few tried to destroy them, but those lights outsmarted them, rolling on the ground, traveling fast.

Years later, Sod and his family didn't pay attention to them anymore. Decided they weren't harmful and accepted them. One day by accident, they were found to have healing properties, and the young and old chased after them for that reason.

Hundreds

A car swerved to the edge of Sugar Martin's farm, and the driver gawked at women picking a field. The driver, Lee Three, knew Sugar Martin's usual getup of black rubber boots, a polka dot sleeveless dress topped with a straw hat. That was weird to make all her pickers wear that same style of clothing.

Three crawled out of the car. He watched. The women reached for a green pepper, and snapped it off the stem, all in the same movement.

The Lady in the Ladybug

He turned away from his audience in the field to answer his phone. "Where are you Reva? The state capitol?"

He turned to face the women, and a dumfounded expression about where they had disappeared to so quickly formed on his lips. Only one woman watched and waited for him to ask her directions or strike up a conversation. He had never talked with Sugar Martin before, only seeing her around town, or in her one food store. Not sure if that was her or one of the pickers, he turned, stuck his long legs and arms inside the small car and sped away, spewing lavender dust.

His small car climbed a hilly road that leveled out to the spacious countryside and came upon a sign on the highway intersection, Glassburgh five miles and San Amez eighty miles; an arrow pointing to the west. He put the car in park at hearing another shrilly ring tone. "Proof? Reva, telling the state officials isn't enough. We have to have video. Missed my chance a few minutes ago. Sugar Martin is strange."

"Strange, how strange?" Reva asked.

Three replied, "Many Sugar Martin's became one Sugar Martin."

"What?"

"I'm not kidding you about that. Gotta drive by another field of hers; see what's going in it."

Welcome to the Farm

"Mother," Razzy hollered, "Where is Chicken Soup?"

Sugar thought a bit before answering, but really asking, "She's not in her roost?"

"No. Since sun up, she's been gone."

"Ohh, Chicken Soup! She likes to—"

"I know." He could hear from memory what Sugar had said about Chicken Soup.

The Lady in the Ladybug

'Chicken Soup likes to poke holes in almost anything, cars, buildings, and people. I like my chicken, but she can be terrible because that Delaware fowl doesn't have a big brain in that large body. Chicken Soup measures the biggest chicken in Sands County, and the largest in the state of Coronado, USA. Chicken Soup is a one of a kind giant— worldwide.'

"This could be bad," Sugar said. She puckered her lips, paused, and sputtered, "The USDA is taking the final soil samples for our organic certification." Her announcement ended with a frown. She gestured at the ground. Her rubber boots had split at the toes.

Razzy shook his head, "Just don't mention it. They may not even see Chicken Soup while they are out here. Why get them scared?"

"You're right. This is a big farm, Chicken Soup could be anywhere." Sugar agreed in a doubtful smile.

Tan with billowing muscles built from years of work on the farm, Razzy hugged his mother and headed to the field to work.

She followed the cement walk along the side of the house, reached for the gate handle on the rose covered fence on the back of the house. Those red roses released a wonderful scent that covered up the smell of natural fertilizer on the garden and fields. Chicken Soup was probably having a feast… somewhere. Sugar's eyebrows furrowed.

Reva

Reva Little stepped up to the receptionist's desk in the lobby of the state building in San Amez.

"USDA director Luke Welch, please?"

The Lady in the Ladybug

The receptionist pressed some buttons on the keyboard. Her polite directions sent Reva across the spacious lobby to the north elevator. "Third floor, turn right. It's on the end of the hall."

Reva stepped away from the desk, but noticed a man hurrying into the building. He dangled his ID badge from a finger, and a suit coat held at the collar by the other hand. He let go of his badge while reaching for the receptionist's hand to shake.

"Pick up your badge off the computer board, now," she said.

His smile fell, removing the badge, looking at her nameplate. "You're new here."

"Yes, this is my first week of employment."

"Hey, Dixon Caddo, and you are— Monterey Montoya. A beautiful name for a beautiful woman."

She smiled. He took off with a wink and stopped at the elevator and gave Monterey another smile. He waved goodbye while Reva stepped inside.

Dix held the elevator door for her. She thanked him and answered her phone. "I'm in the elevator, Luke."

Dix turned his head toward her. Luke was his boss. He stepped slightly closer and opened his mouth, but decided it best to keep quiet. This woman was really dressed up to see the USDA's head man. Wondered what she was? An elected official? Her perfume was pretty strong, and that long brown hair swirled around her shoulders like a fur collar.

The elevator stopped. He waited a second and that woman stepped out going toward the end of the hall where Luke Welch, supervisor of the USDA, occupied his office overlooking San Amez. Dix watched her walk like she was late to the appointment and rush right into his office.

"Reva, glad you made it," Luke said.

She scrutinized his lazy nod at the chair in front of his desk.

"Here is the disc with all my findings on it." She sat, crossing her legs. "Oh, and a piece of the original asteroid."

"Really." He took the small plastic sack off her palm.

"Really. It is packed with information. Discovered that healing mineral."

"How?"

"The vegetables that grow in the asteroid soil are the most beneficial, it prevents disease, and even cures some diseases," she said, leaning in closer. "People in Sands County are the healthiest in the state of Coronado, maybe even the world."

"Oh, I don't believe that. Every place on earth has disease."

"Read the report, Luke. Plus, my partner, Lee Three, said he when he passed Sugar Martin's farm late last evening, he saw weird lights. He also said she divided—"

"I don't want silly reports, we need hard evidence."

"I'll get it for you." Reva smiled, blew him a hefty kiss, and left his office. She checked her cell phone and waited for the elevator door to open.

Monterey caught a bit of her phone conversation on her way out, "We're going to get rich from this, Lee."

Malvin, Dix, and Jo, USDA agents

USDA agent, Dix Caddo, picked up mail addressed to him, heard Jo on the phone and Malvin at the copy machine. His favorite cup was clean and close to the coffee maker. Filling it, he sat and listened to Mal and Jo's conversation.

He plopped in a chair and put his feet up on Jo's desk in front of him. She swatted them off. The buzzer interrupted their ritual, and Jo's courteous voice produced, "Yes, sir."

11

The Lady in the Ladybug

Dix and Mal interpreted her facial expressions on what Director Welch wanted.

"Sands County." She confirmed what he said and eyed Mal. "Records for the past 50 years? Sure, no problem."

"Fifty years? He's kidding," Dix said, watching Mal strut into the records room.

Jo reminded Dix, "It's all on microfilm."

She grinned when Mal set the film on Dix's desk.

"Not much work," Mal said, looking down at him.

Dix stared up at Jo and over at Mal. "No, I am not," he whined.

"Director Welch assigned Mal and me to maps, so— best get to it."

"Okay, what I am searching for?"

"Inspections of farms in Sands County, and anything unusual."

Dix folded his arms across his chest. "Unusual?"

"That's what he requested. Unusual."

He sighed on standing and picked up the small box. He dragged a chair up to the desk, and pulled out a foot of film. He snapped the roll in place and wrapped the excess over and under the glass plate. Grumbling at trying to secure the end spool, he read, "January nineteen fifty nine."

Jo typed on her computer keyboard, hit enter and up came satellite readings of Sands County on the monitor. She printed that and handed it to Mal.

He put the print on a copy machine, tapped some buttons, and a larger picture rolled out onto a tray. Mal studied that larger print and pointed out one particular spot. Jo shrugged.

"Whoa," Dix exclaimed, rubbing his hand over his short black hair. He hit print and out came a copy. He let it dry and took it to the copy machine.

"What?" Jo asked. She looked eagerly at the copy Dix put in front of her. "That's unusual."

She handed the copy to Mal.

"That's weird."

12

The Lady in the Ladybug

Dix returned to the microfiche. "What?" He bent forward, almost nose touching the screen.

Jo and Mal turned their heads. Dix hit the print button again. He sat back, tapping fingers on the chair arm. "That's impossible. Whoever reported this must have been smoking some ditch weed."

"Have either of you ever been to Sands County or Glassburgh?" Jo asked.

"No, not me. I'm from northern California," Mal said.

"Ya don't look like a California boy," Dix said.

"Well, where're you from?" Mal retorted.

"Missouri""

"Funny, you don't look like a hillbilly."

"Boys, all I wanted to know was—"

"No," Mal said.

"No, what about you, Jo?"

"Yes, I've been there. An asteroid hit one hundred years ago in that area, the dust from this asteroid mixed in with the soil over time, and when this mixture is churned up from everyday living, farming, or the wind, it rises into the air and creates a lavender haze."

The phone buzzed. Jo answered. "Yes, sir, I called Sugar Martin yesterday. Her farm is due for second soil tests for organic certification. We will," she said to Welch, ending the short conversation. She searched the computer for the records of her farm. "Here's your chance, Mal, Dix, to see Glassburgh, the home of the lavender haze. We have the assignment for soil samples, Welch wants it done today."

She proceeded to the file cabinet and pulled out a packet named simply, organic soil certification.

Mal tightened his tie, combed his sandy hair, and gathered his papers. Dix turned off the microfilm machine and darted to the door. Jo rolled on pink lipstick, and pushed her chair close to her desk. Mal motioned for her to walk ahead of him. She nodded at his courteous ways.

The Lady in the Ladybug

Dix beat the others into the elevator, and held the door open.

At the lobby, Dix aimed himself at the pretty receptionist who chuckled at the wall painting. "You are here," she said, and read out loud the text below the mural.

Coronado, the short and chubby state below the panhandle of
Oklahoma
and shoulder-to-shoulder with northeastern
New Mexico
borders the Canadian River. Texas is the neighbor to the south.

On the west side of Coronado, the capital of San Amez, the many mountains in the city and points of importance were printed in English and Spanish. Glassburgh was on the right side of the map. In small font below it read *City of Lavender*.

Jo passed the receptionist desk first, and then Mal. The receptionist turned when hearing their footsteps and sat at her desk. Dix stopped. She typed on her computer keyboard, as if she were checking them out of the building.

"We're going across the state, Monterey, see you tomorrow," he said. He lingered at the desk admiring her blonde hair in a lavish bun, bronze skin, and a set of perfect white teeth. He took off with a wink "I'll bring you back some lavender soil."

"I bet that'll smell good."

Dix only laughed.

When entering the garage, Dix always got the keys before anyone else had the chance to drive to assignments. The garage attendant seemed to always toss the keys to him after the tenth time of him pushing his way to the desk. This car checked out to him was a plain white sedan. Dix eyed it, rubbing his chin, "Not quite what I wanted to drive."

The Lady in the Ladybug

The traffic was sparse on the street he took, but at the intersection ahead, it seemed the entire city wanted to use that street. That street curved around a mountain, and to the right, Dix exited to the highway that led to Sands County.

An hour and fifteen minutes of silence abruptly ended. Dix pointed ahead. "Look at that big hill." He said and checked the map unfolded across the steering wheel.

Mal squinted at Dix's foot on the gas pedal.

"Speed to the top of the hill, let off the gas, and feel the rush." Dix grinned. The car quickly gained speed to the crest.

Jo grabbed hold of the armrest; Mal closed his eyes.

"Wahoo!" Dix hooted over the hill. Like a huge poster in front of them, that was the farm they were sent to gather final soil samples for organic certification; a farm that grew in the middle of Sands County, Coronado, five miles from Glassburgh.

Coasting to the bottom, Dix drove slowly and looked at the luscious leafy rows of cauliflower that went on and on forever. In the lavender haze, the large, leafy green broccoli grew into a wonderland. Large artichokes dotted the landscape.

A half mile more, watermelons grew on the left side of the road and cantaloupe on the right. Dix lay on the brakes, tires screeched, and he rolled down the window. They did expect the vegetables and fruits to grow large on this organic farm, but quite didn't anticipate them over growing in size. Jo squinted out the window, trying to determine the size of that huge watermelon out in the field.

Dix approached the sign marked Marquez Road and turned. A mile-long rock road ended and a white Cape Cod influenced house came into view. Dix parked on the shoulder of the road, because it was policy not to drive on grass. Jo crawled out of the backseat, smoothed her twisted brown silky pleated skirt, and tugged her yellow knit top with USDA embroidered in red over the breast. She pulled several questionnaires out of the manila envelope on the backseat of the government car. She put those inside one folder, clicked an ink pen, and reminded Dix and Mal to clip on their ID badges. Dix spit shined his badge. Mal reached into the backseat and picked up two long clear tubes.

"I like the lavender haze, and soil," Jo said.

"Eerie, like a science fiction movie," Dix said, looking over the land.

Mal glanced at the horizon. "Creepy," he said trailing behind Jo and Dix onto the cement walk that forked. On the left, the sidewalk continued into the fenced in backyard. They chose the right path. It led them to the front of the house and to the front cement stoop. Dix rang the doorbell. They waited. Dix rang it one more time. "Jo, didn't Mrs. Martin say she would be home?"

They stepped off the stoop and turned, walked around the house and stopped.

A woman waited with hands on hips. She was a large woman with a large bosom and hips inside a knee length brown and white polka dot dress. Large rubber boots about size eleven ripped at the toes and her floppy straw hat fitted loosely on her head.

Watching the three USDA employees stare at her, she smiled and extended her hand.

"Sugar Martin, welcome to my farm."

Jo stepped forward and took her hand, feeling her firm grip. "Hello, Ms. Martin, I'm Jo Harris from the USDA. This is Mal Fordors and Dix Caddo." Mal and Dix nodded respectively. "We have several questionnaires to fill out."

Sugar curled her index finger at them. "Come on over to the cornfield, and then we'll fly over to the orchard."

Jo nodded and took off behind Sugar. "Ms. Martin, how long have you been farming?" she asked, now trotting beside her.

"All my life, since I was a child. Papa was a corn farmer, and mama raised a garden."

The Lady in the Ladybug

Sugar motioned them on and they followed her to the higher than an elephant's eye cornfield. Sugar paused and put a hand to her ear. A squeak and pop echoed through the fields.

"Listening to the corn growing?" Dix asked, amused.

She smiled sincerely, and led them to the back of the house to the tomatoes growing inside wooden cages. The ground sloped up to the horizon revealing them planted in a diamond pattern.

Mal stepped closer to the first row of tomatoes. He pointed at a huge tomato.

"Un—believ—able," he stammered.

"How did you—" Dix asked.

Jo searched on the questionnaires for the category of 'what do we classify it?'

Sugar proudly smiled at her large tomatoes as round as a dinner plate, and tugged one off a vine. She handed the shiny red tomato to Mal who grabbed it with both hands.

"Just bite into that juicy baby," she said.

Mal wiped a spot off the tomato on his shirt. He chomped down, spilling juice over his arm, "Uhmmmm—delicious!"

He passed it over to Jo. She nibbled off a bite, and said while chewing, "Y'u can grow— a mean tomato."

Sugar fluttered her eyelids, unsure of what that meant, watching Jo hand the tomato over to Dix. He took one big bite. "Mmm–mmm–mmm."

"Sugar," Jo said, "To grow your large produce, you obviously pick off blooms, only leaving one to grow large, is that correct?"

"No. All my produce grows large, it always has."

Mal raised his eyebrows. "You disk any special additives into the soil?"

Sugar shook her head no. Mal pushed down one six-inch long tube into the soil, twisting and turning it until he packed it with dirt.

He extracted the tube and capped it off, writing the date on the cap.

The Lady in the Ladybug

Jo sorted the papers. "It says here you have two stores?"

Sugar shifted her weight and pulled her floppy hat back into a comfortable place on her head. "I have one store in Glassburgh, and just acquired another."

"Both 'n Glassburgh?" Dix asked, finishing off one side of the tomato.

"Correct."

"What do people around here think about the lavender haze?" Mal asked, hand up at the sky.

"It's been lavender as long as I remember, and as long as Papa remembered."

"Doesn't it seem weird?" Dix asked, squinting.

Sugar shrugged. "Everyone just accepts it."

"Anything else weird around here?" Mal asked.

"Uhmmm, no," Sugar said, watching Jo put the questionnaires inside the manila folder. "We're done here. Now we need to go to your orchard—" Jo paused, wondering why Sugar stomped the ground with one foot.

"Cleopatra!" Sugar shouted.

"Who's that?" Jo asked.

Sugar pointed. There they saw a huge red object lift out of the cornfield. It hummed overhead and landed between the tomatoes and cornfield. Jo, Dix, and Mal laughed at the huge electronic ladybug.

Sugar retorted with a 'humph' and walked ten feet to the lettuce row and tore off a leaf like a sheet of paper out of a notebook. She made sure the three government inspectors watched her when she fed the leaf the size of Jo's questionnaires to Cleopatra.

"Good Cleopatra, good girl," Sugar said.

"Ms. Martin," Dix said. "The three of us have worked for the government for many years in many areas. Nothing much surprises us anymore. Anyone with a lot of money could have an electronic ladybug built."

The Lady in the Ladybug

Sugar shook her head and tapped on the ladybug's shiny shell. "Do you hear an echo? Cleopatra is real! You are standing on a one hundred percent organic farm. The soil, you will find, is pure and virgin. I have spent years on growing large and selling large—it takes dedication and—"

"Ms. Martin," Dix interrupted crisply.

Sugar pointed to the ladybug. "We are flying to the orchard; Cleopatra is waiting."

"Fly? How?" Jo asked.

"Under her wings," Sugar said, raising her arms.

Cleopatra raised her red outer shell and stretched out wings. She lifted straight up and hovered over the four people. Dix tried to run, but the inner wing closed on him, pushing him against the ladybug's body. "Hey! Call off your ladybug!"

Jo wrapped her arms over her head, whimpering. "Get away. Shoo!"

"Hey, lady! Get this thing off us. Now!" Mal struck a pose of a boxer, punching at the strong wing.

Sugar yelled instructions, ignoring their pleading and cursing. "Grab hold of a vein in the wing closest to her body. That one doesn't move. Plant your feet on a lower vein, the inner wing will hold you in tightly. We're taking off in a few seconds."

"I'm stuck! I can't move! This is crazy!" Mal yelled.

"This woman *is* crazy!" Dix shouted.

"Don't worry, she's as solid as a 747," Sugar hollered, holding onto a vein. "It's a bit uncomfortable during the first flight. You'll get used to it."

"Why would we want to get used to it?" Mal asked, hearing Jo screaming as Cleopatra buzzed into the sky. They caught sight of Sugar tucked in behind the translucent wings. Those wings wrapped around their bodies like a cross between a Venus Fly Trap and a grandma's homemade quilt.

Jo felt herself slide, finding nothing to stop her feet. "I'm falling out!"

"Cleopatra hasn't lost a passenger yet!" Sugar yelled back.

Dix punched a hole through the wing, and stuck his head through it and yelled at Sugar. "When we get back to the office, you're going to the loony bin!"

Sugar pouted. Pulling a vein, signaling stop, Cleopatra and she landed softly. Jo, Dix, and Mal stumbled away.

"This place is freaking crazy. Wait till we tell Welch all about this!" Dix snarled, sliding his hand over his hair.

Mal stuck the second tube deep into the dirt. "We need to finish our business and turn in the samples. Get us back to our car," he demanded, extracting and capping the tube.

Jo pulled her skirt in place and turned. She stared at a skyscraper of glass glistening in the sunshine down in the valley. "Is that Glassburgh?"

"It is," said Sugar.

"Okay, Ms. Martin, which direction is your freaky farm? We need to get back to the car." Dix grumbled.

Sugar batted away tears. "Three miles back … on this road."

"C'mon, Jo, Mal," Dix said, strutting away.

Jo stepped over to Sugar and shook her hand. "I'll mail you the decision of organic certification as soon as the results are in."

Sugar smiled confidently. "I know they will certify me."

"Let's hope so," Jo said, pulling her hands out of Sugar's large fingers.

"We hope so too, because, we are not coming back here," Dix hollered.

The three USDA workers marched down the road, cursing the day, wishing they didn't have this assignment.

"There is something wrong with this lavender haze," Mal said to Dix.

"Yeah, something weird is in it."

"Must be some mineral that makes things grow big," Jo said.

"Why hasn't someone stumbled upon this farm before? Wrote about it in some magazine?" Mal asked.

"Mal," Dix whined, "Who would believe it?"

Their voices became less audible as they briskly walked the road away from Sugar. She took in what they were saying about the farm, watching them become smaller and smaller down the road, like three ants scurrying over their ant hill.

After the USDA agents were gone, Sugar signaled Cleopatra and she raised her wings and scooped Sugar under, lifting effortlessly and buzzing over fields of large cabbages, beets, and leeks. Cleopatra flew above the cars on the highway, above the people walking downtown, and landed on the park across the street from Squarestone Enterprises.

Cleopatra fit in. She rested beside the elephant slide and turtle sandbox. A little girl ran to the ladybug first, tried to climb it, but proved too slippery. She stared into Cleopatra's huge eyes. A woman wearing a pink T-shirt, Levi's and pink cap caught up with the girl.

The *Walk* light turned green and Sugar proceeded across the street, and onto the sidewalk beside the old Squarestone Hotel, now Squarestone Enterprises.

At the entrance of the large stone building, the handsome door attendant held the door open for her.

"Thank you, young man." She tromped over the Italian tile of the spacious lobby and paused at the two-tiered fountain in the center. She heard chiming on the opening of the elevator door nine feet away. Out came executives in black suits and expensive shoes. Passing, they gawked, but politely greeted her.

Sugar entered the open elevator and boarded, punching five, and hung on to the rail, her eyes tightly closed as the elevator raised.

The door opened unto a large office with a young receptionist who instantly buzzed when she saw Sugar walk past. The receptionist alerted the people in the glass-enclosed offices by knocking on the windows and pointing.

A tall handsome man came out of an office to stop her.

"Sugar, please have a seat in my office. I'm on a long distance call, but I should be with you shortly."

"Oh, I'm not in a hurry, Chris" she said, walking into his office.

Another receptionist pushed a refreshment cart piled high with fruit and cookies, and carafes of coffee and tea. Sugar plopped on the leather couch, reaching for cookies. She nodded thanks to the receptionist pouring her a glass of tea and the welcome taste of homemade cookies.

Chris Tatro peeked around the door at her, smiled and winked.

Sugar wiped crumbs off her cheek and extended her hand for the expected handshake.

"Always a pleasure, Sugar," he said.

"Everyone is so excited to see me when I come in."

Chris sat and took one cookie. "Well, you are one of a kind."

Sugar embarrassingly agreed, and poured a cup of tea for Chris. "Thank you." He set it on the floor.

She raised her eyebrows and slyly looked at it. Chris picked up the cup and set it on the coffee table.

"Well, the USDA took final samples for my organic certification."

"Did they?" He sat back on the couch.

"Nice people, though, I don't think they liked the ladybug ride."

Chris covered his mouth and snickered.

A pretty secretary came in with papers clasped together, handed a pen to Sugar, and she signed her name on the lines indicated as CEO of Sugar Martin Enterprises. With another organic food store in Glassburgh, one on the other side of town, the glassless side, and now one near the glass skyscrapers, Sugar had franchised.

"Here is the key, Sugar, shall we go? We'll make floor plans," Chris said, opening the door for her. Sugar walked into the view of the people in the offices. They watched she and Chris board the elevator, and Sugar grab hold of the car's railing. She closed her eyes.

"Sugar, you fly in a ladybug and you are afraid in the elevator?"

"Not afraid. That sudden stopping sensation gets me every time."

They walked out of the lobby of Squarestone Enterprises and out to a blue convertible parked on the street. He opened the door for her and shut it after she settled down onto the seat. He took off around the car when his cell phone rang. He listened, sputtered a few words, and tried to cut in on the person speaking to him. "Just a minute, please." He held the cell phone away from him. "Sugar, I have a contract issue with a client upstairs. It won't take long."

Sugar nodded, knowing it would take time. She realized it felt good to be sitting, even if it was in a convertible on a warm day. She watched the traffic, snuggling down in the car, letting her floppy hat shade her from the hot sun. Her eyes closed and soon she felt sleep creeping in. The farm was dark but light. Fuzzy images became clearer, and a watermelon rolled down a hill, and her son, Razzy chased it. Cleopatra chased it. She chased it. Heading toward the house, it became the target for the runaway watermelon. Smack!

Smacked into the house and the watermelon exploded. Everyone sat around a picnic table eating a huge piece of the watermelon. People she didn't know were eating with her, and picking out seeds the size of a dinner plate. She picked one up and looked at herself in the seed's reflection. She tried to dig a hole to plant the seeds. She dug and dug and...

She woke herself, snorting at the end of a long snore. Looking at her watch, she had been asleep for forty-five minutes? Chris was still inside working out a contract problem? Must be some problem. She exited the car and went inside. She asked the door attendant if Chris was still upstairs. He pressed a button on a phone. "Is Chris Tatro there?" He looked up at Sugar. "He is."

"When he comes this way, tell him I'll be waiting for him across the street at the park."

23

"Will do," he said.

At the water fountain, Sugar filled a little cup and took a long drink, and dabbed a little water on her face. She fluttered her eyelashes, and squinted. "Cleopatra!" Sugar trotted out of the building and at the curb she saw that her ladybug still waited in the park, and no one bothered her. She pressed the *Walk* button on the post, but she decided she needed something more to drink. The convenience store that used to be a café was open. The new door and windows sparkled; the new marquee shined bright with the price of a gallon of milk in black. Only a few cars were parked in front, a motorcycle, a newer gold car, a blue pickup, and a white sedan with the red letters of USDA on the doors.

The trunk was open about three inches, one door ajar, and a flat tire on the back. Peeking inside, her soil samples were uncapped and spilled across the seat. The papers and the manila envelopes Jo filled out a couple hours ago were scattered over the backseat, and her nametag was left behind.

Sugar noticed paint had been scratched off in a crisscross pattern on the top, and dents and deeper scratches sliced the hood. What could have done that?

"Chicken! Soup!"

She took four long steps to the front door of the store and entered. Around the seating area and over to the video section, she paraded through the four aisles. Sugar presented herself in front of the cashier and asked the young man if he remembered one woman and two men coming inside. She described Jo's yellow green knit top with the letters USDA in a red appliqué.

"No." He ripped open a carton of cigarettes.

She placed both hands on the counter. "Perhaps they bought some things with a government credit card? Do you remember that?"

"No." He inserted the packs in spring-loaded compartments.

The Lady in the Ladybug

Sugar tapped both hands on the counter, hoping it would rouse his memory. "Do you know anything about the white car out front with the flat tire?"

"Uh, no, I don't."

She pulled her hands back, looking worried. She walked out of the store, taking one last look at the car, and curious if Chris was looking for her. She hurried back to his car, and just then, he walked out of Squarestone Enterprises.

Sugar plopped her hands on her hips. "Chris, the USDA car is over at the convenience store, damaged, and Jo, Mal and Dix are not around, anywhere."

"I bet they're around somewhere," he said, chuckling.

"My soil sample is spilled. They wouldn't let that happen."

"It's not like they can't get more soil."

"Call 911."

Chris rolled his eyes and flipped open his phone and handed it to her.

"This is Sugar Martin and I'm worried. Three government inspectors came to my farm this afternoon, and now their car is damaged in front of the convenience store on Turnage Street, and they are *not* around, anywhere." Sugar walked to the car. "That would be great if you would send an officer."

Chris looked at his watch, and paced the sidewalk. He looked at his wristwatch several times. Sugar watched the street corner for a patrol car. "They probably called a taxi," Chris said.

Officer Teresa Talamantes introduced herself, and walked around the vehicle. She called in the tag number. "It'll take a few minutes."

Sugar looked into the car again until Chris and the officer commented on the hood. "Wow, took something strong to make those scratches," Chris said.

Officer Talamantes shook her head, agreeing. A voice on her pager said, "No one reported any accidents with that tag number."

25

"Good," Sugar said, and they departed the government car abandoned.

Grabbing for the alarm clock, Sugar sent a photo frame to the floor. She picked up the wood frame with a picture of a younger and smaller Chicken Soup. After setting it back on the nightstand, she grabbed her red housecoat and hurried into the kitchen. Razzy slurped the last of his coffee from his favorite cup and grabbed the doorknob about to depart the house.

"Chicken Soup?" she asked.

"Going to go look now."

Her shoulders slumped at the disappointment and watched Razzy walk out of the house and over to Chicken Soup's thicket of Pampas grass. He spent a few seconds in it and exited, looking around.

"Where is that Delaware fowl?" Sugar grumbled, and hurried to the shower, spent ten minutes in it, and donned another polka dot dress and black rubber boots, brand new. She popped outside, and followed Razzy across the backyard with a large sack of chicken feed balancing his shoulder.

"Razzy, I'll look for her to the south, you go north."

Sugar stomped the ground. She looked up. Out of the cornfield Cleopatra hovered and landed next to Sugar. She grabbed a vein and planted her feet on a lower vein, remembering her first experience of ladybug riding.

Back in high school, Sugar crawled over, around, and under a huge ladybug; tickling her belly and looking into those enormous eyes. That Cleopatra raised her shell to take flight and Sugar grabbed hold of a vein in the wing closest to her body, and planted her feet on a lower vein. The middle set of wings closed on her, and up into the air they went, thrust by outer wings.

The Lady in the Ladybug

Sugar screamed terrified vowel sounds the entire flight from the backyard to the cornfield. She fell out near Papa on the corn picker. She pulled herself up off the ground, seeing Papa's eyes wide-open in shock.

Training sessions daily, Cleopatra seemed to understand words that came with the commands.

On the edge of her farm, near the windbreak next to Mrs. Bandstra's two-story house, two large white feathers dangled from a branch. "Down." She commanded and Cleopatra glided to the ground, releasing Sugar. She straightened her polka dot dress and straw hat into place. She took a deep breath, "Chicken Soup!" She yelled. She didn't anticipate a reply.

"Over here!" a man shouted.

"Bring a gun!" another man screamed.

Sugar gasped. She stepped around the trees and stumps, holes and wash-outs, and walked through as carefully she could to the voices. She discerned there were two males and one female frantically pleading, taunting, bullying, and bribing Chicken Soup. "I'm here!" Sugar let out.

Chicken Soup charged out of the trees and squawked at Cleopatra.

Sugar flipped her phone open. "Razzy, I found her, Cleopatra is on her way home, got scared of Chicken Soup."

"Sugar?" The female voice asked.

Seeing the silky pleated skirt tattered and torn, she replied, "Hello. Help is coming."

"Don't tell me that is your chicken," Dix said.

"Had Chicken Soup since she was an egg," Sugar said, stepping closer.

"It doesn't mind well," Jo said, watching the chicken snuggle up to Sugar.

"How long have you been here in the tree?"

"Since yesterday, after we talked to you," Jo said.

Sugar pondered that a few seconds. "All that time in this tree?"

27

"Yep," Dix said. "Out here all night, no water, no food, no sleep, just trying to keep away from that monster."

"Oh, I'm so sorry." She flipped open her cell phone once again, and instructed Razzy to come over to the Bandstra place and take Chicken Soup to the barn. Sugar ended her call to Razzy and looked sadly up into the trees. "I do apologize for this. I will take all of you to my home." Sugar nudged Chicken Soup, trying to push her away from the trees.

Dix smirked. "I don't think so. We'll be on our way to San Amez."

Mal spoke up. "In what? Some deaf idiot towed the car away." He looked down at Sugar and grinned, "We sure aren't calling our boss." He turned to Dix, "Sugar's accommodations will be accepted."

Jo agreed. "A hot bath."

"A cup of coffee, mmm," Mal said

Sugar held her face in her hands while the trio named the things they wanted after the harrowing night of the chicken. Surely, they could have snuck away at some point. "Couldn't you…" Sugar thought it best not to ask now.

She tried to push Chicken Soup out of way so the USDA inspectors could descend the trees, but Chicken Soup flapped her wings, and stabbed the trees with her sharp beak. Sugar flailed arms and let her alone. "When she's angry, I can't do anything with her."

"We didn't provoke her," Mal said.

"It's just the way she is, the larger they are, the meaner they become." Looking up at Cleopatra hovering above the chicken, a rope dropped and lowered until it was above her head. Wearing chaps, spurs, leather gloves, a striped shirt and football helmet, Razzy landed onto Chicken Soup's back. He wrapped the rope around her big neck and pulled, maneuvering Chicken Soup out of the windbreak and onto the open field.

Dix slowly climbed down the tree. Mal inched his way down,

strategically placing his feet on the sturdiest branch.

"Thank goodness for Razzy," Sugar said.

Cleopatra landed, and plucked for herself a long slender tendril of young asparagus.

"These aren't trees? This is asparagus! We stayed all night in a gigantic asparagus patch?" Dix said, helping Jo down the last few feet of the asparagus stalk.

"Are you surprised?" Jo asked him.

"No, not really."

Sugar's brows furrowed, and looked down. "Please, let's go to my house for breakfast. You will need to get another soil sample for your boss."

Mal stepped forward, nursing a tightened muscle in his back. "How do you know?" he snapped.

Sugar fluttered her eyelashes, fighting back tears. "I found your car in Glassburgh, and the soil sample uncapped."

Jo shut her eyes tightly. "Let's go to your house." Making a face, trying to endure another ladybug ride, she walked into the field. Sugar waved Mal and Dix to the field.

Cleopatra's outer shell rose. Her inner wings lifted and swept the people close to her body. Jo screamed. Sugar assured her once more that Cleopatra could not lose passengers.

"The wings are like Velcro and only if you were naked, would you fall out."

Jo stopped screaming and began laughing.

Cleopatra landed softly on a patch of grass near the house, and Sugar led her guests to the unlocked door. Jo walked in first with Dix and Mal trailing behind. The house was completely normal. White walls with blue trim and blue carpet met them in the front living room, which led to the kitchen of yellow walls, and wood grained vinyl flooring. New appliances sparkled beside a clean uncluttered countertop. Jo read down a shopping list clipped onto a round metal magnet.

Dix and Mal sat at the kitchen table and watched the food that Sugar took from the fridge and cupboard. The bacon and eggs sizzled in the frying pan. Sugar poured pancake batter in after the eggs and bacon were scooped out of the pan.

The aroma of coffee rolled over the breakfast table, and in a few minutes, a plate full of food plopped down in front of each of Sugar's guests.

Mal and Dix looked very pleased and stuck their eating utensils into the thick pancakes.

They quickly ate, raving over them to Sugar. They consumed every bit on their plates. Every crumb was wiped off all the plates, sparkling better than if just washed.

"That was the best tasting food I have ever eaten," Mal said.

Sugar let a smile come, "It's all organic, that's why," she said. "Oh, but I don't have my organic certificate, so—I guess I can't say it is certified organic."

"We'll work on that," said Dix, winking.

Sugar picked up the dishes and stacked them in the sink. She looked out the window. Jo yawned.

Mal looked at a picture of a girl in a pumpkin patch.

"Is that you as a child?" he asked.

"Why, yes, I was helping papa with the harvest." She stood by the picture, fondly looking at the picture of him.

"Here, on this farm?" he asked.

"Yes. Where else?" She asked, chuckling.

"Sugar, this farm isn't like the rest of the world. Fruits and vegetables grow smaller, much smaller."

"I know. I have worked hard developing my large produce. Just ask anyone in Glassburgh about me, they'll back me up." Her eyes teared. "My mother and father and I all worked together on this farm all my life until my mother and father grew old. Papa knew all about organic farming, and why not, everybody was an organic grower a long time ago. You had to be or starve.

My father learned from his father, and then his father, and now I know all the secrets of growing big and selling big. I sold from my own little corner by a gas station in Glassburgh, until Squarestone Enterprises took an interest in me, and they asked me to be in business with them. They bought a building, then another, on both sides of town."

Jo and Mal nodded. Dix folded his arms over his chest, unsure.

"Let's go to town and get the car, Glassburgh, is it?" Mal said.

"That means another ladybug ride," Jo said.

"No, I'll have Razzy drive you." Sugar reached for her cell phone and texted.

Dix pulled out of a pocket the satellite imagery map with all the roads and highways of Sands County and studied it. He showed it to Sugar. "Where are we?"

She circled her big finger over the map and touched the spot. She noticed no wedding rings on Dix or Mal.

"Are any of you married?" Sugar eyed their hands.

"I am," said Jo.

"Nope," said Dix.

"Mal?" Sugar asked.

"Uh, no, recently unengaged."

"Oh, too bad." Sugar finished the text and rinsed the last pan in the sink and piled it on top the others in the dish drainer.

Dix, Mal, and Jo watched her, hoping she would share her status with them.

Sugar remained quiet.

Jo yawned.

Sugar offered her rest in her bedroom, not knowing how soon Razzy would be there. Jo accepted.

Sugar showed the way, and closed the bedroom door on her way out. Jo sank into the soft mattress, swallowed up in the soft stuffing.

The Lady in the Ladybug

She turned to her side, facing the wall filled with pictures. There were photos, new and old, and Jo saw a young and beautiful Sugar in a beauty contest.

She was very fit and toned, muscular in a feminine way. She had long blonde hair in a high ponytail. She was a beauty queen wearing the crown and holding a dozen roses. On the ribbon around her was written in gold glitter, Miss Sands County. Printed in bold on the photo—Miss Roxy Roxalena Wins Beauty Pageant.

So that's not Sugar?

She haphazardly glanced over the other pictures. There she was again on her wedding day. Roxy Roxalena married Hugh Martin from Houston, Texas.

Okay, her real name is Roxy? Sugar is just a nickname?

A picture farther away was a baby picture. "Razzy Martin. Oh my gosh, that was her son!"

At the very top of the wall of pictures was the front page of the Glassburgh Gazette. Jo rolled out of bed and stood on a chair. The cover story was Roxy Roxalena, county wrestler. She had taken first place at the county fair for the fifth year in a row and had gained national attention. A pro wrestling manager from New York City signed her to perform with the other pro wrestlers.

"Sugar a wrestler? This is wild," she whispered.

Jo imagined a wrestling match in New York City. An announcer blasts out over the loud speaker, 'And now, the sensation we've been waiting for, the county fair wrestling champion, the beautiful, the awesome, Roxy Roxalena!'

She strutted out with arms over her head, showing off her strong arms and legs. The crowd applauded and whistled. Roxy took her place in the ring and waited for her opponent, the fiercely dreaded — dreaded, uh, she couldn't think of a name for her. She looked over the other newspaper clippings in frames.

Someone knocked; Sugar called her name.

Jo stepped off the chair and dropped onto the bed. "Yes, Sugar?"

The door opened all the way. Sugar announced that Razzy was here.

"Okay, I'm ready." Jo walked out behind Sugar, now the most fascinating woman in Sands County.

Cleopatra and Chicken Soup

Along Marquis Road, the two giants of the farm scoured the ground. Chicken Soup trailed a line of ants, pecking the ground, but really hitting the soft, wet earth with her beak, slinging grass up and over. A fat worm wriggled up out of the ground; Chicken Soup darted for it, missing it by an inch.

Cleopatra's lurch at it won her the prize.

Angry at the loss, Chicken Soup pecked Cleopatra's shell. She zipped up into the sky, landed behind Chicken Soup, and stuck out her sharp pincer. She nipped tail feathers, sending Chicken Soup fluttering and flapping across the yard.

Cleopatra's shadow passed over, and Sugar looked up. A feather floated down to her boots.

"Fighting again." Chicken Soup was always the loser.

Around the corner of the house to catch up with her large pet, Sugar stood in front of Cleopatra.

Through those huge eyes, Cleopatra watched Sugar lift her foot and put it down, a little perturbed. As always, Cleopatra opened her red shell waiting for Sugar to grab hold.

Sugar pulled feathers out of her mouth.

"Bad Cleopatra!"

The Lady in the Ladybug

Her outer shell closed and lowered to the ground. Sugar shook her finger at her. "Don't play dead... you know what you did." Playing dead got her out of a lot of trouble.

Returning to yard work, and following a trail of feathers, she heard peeps. She took a few steps closer to the road, the garage, and the barn. Smaller down feathers rolled around the thicket.

Sugar slipped into Chicken Soup's hideaway, walking on layers of pampas grass from many autumns past. Now the pampas blooms entangled at the top. Inside, a short foyer led to a crooked path to the main living area.

Three yellow chicks snuggled each other. Their little orange beaks opened and closed during their nap, chests rose and fell. Plump webbed feet wiggled in their dreams of pulling worms and chasing grasshoppers. Chicken Soup ran in, and pushed her way to the chicks. Sugar stumbled out of the way, but still watched.

Chicken Soup bent down and nuzzled each chick with her beak. After snuggling down beside them, her eyes grew heavy.

Sugar smiled and backed out of the thicket hearing *Sluirt.* That familiar sound of pulling a spoonful of gelatin out of a mold. *Sluirt.*

"Ladybug babies."

Sluirt

Globs of yellow oozed out of the wet sloppy earth in the pumpkin patch. Seven baby ladybugs marched out of the patch. They had no spots on their shells, not until they were adults, and their legs carried each one like little soldiers. All seven, no, all eight baby ladybugs.

"Babies everywhere! I love it!"

Sugar adjusted her floppy hat. "I'm going to need help."

The Lady in the Ladybug

Bobby Click

Round plump fairytale looking pumpkins just didn't grow that way, they developed from patience. It didn't take much time in one day to cinderellaize the pumpkins.

In the six long rows, Sugar turned the young pumpkins onto their bottoms, and following along, Cleopatra chomping down the smaller pumpkins. Tagging along behind were her young ladybugs just hatched, crawling over everything in their path.

"You know, Cleopatra? It is four months till Halloween. Then winter, ugh, time to hibernate."

Hearing a rumble, Sugar watched a white pickup slowly humming down the road. Sugar noticed new clean tires, like shoes on the first day of school. The pickup pulled to the shoulder, the shiny window on the passenger side slid down halfway.

"Ms. Martin? Bobby Click. I called you a couple days back about help on your farm."

She stepped closer to the window, peering down inside. "Yes, I remember."

"Exactly what would I be… doing?" he asked, watching the young ladybugs march across the road.

"Just that," she pointed. "Keeping track of the young, not letting them eat the crops. I also have—"

"Those real? Not robots?" He stared.

Sugar tilted her hat back so it would not bump the window. "Yes, everything on my farm grows big."

"I never have been a ladybug cowboy."

Sugar smiled slightly. She rubbed her cheek, looking him over, judging his character. Clean cut; smelled nice.

"You're a native?" she asked.

"Yes, born and reared in Sands County."

"Reared, my, you also use correct grammar," Sugar said, smiling.

"Had to, my mother was a teacher."

"I could use someone full-time, but part-time— I'm willing to give you a go of it."

A big smile came over Bobby, showing Sugar that he accepted. Bobby shook her large hand.

Chicken Soup swooped down, eyeball on the windshield, nostrils flaring, steaming up the glass.

Bobby squinted several times, not letting himself believe what he saw. He watched a huge ladybug pincer down the straggling weeds between rows of pumpkins, and her young did the same. A huge chicken ran toward her chicks and tracked down bugs and grasshoppers.

"Yes, you are seeing a huge chicken," Sugar said, adjusting her floppy hat. "This is Chicken Soup and she has three chicks, large and playful. Your job, Bobby, is not to let them eat the ladybug babies."

Bobby grabbed the door handle and spilled out of the pickup. He stared into Sugar's eyes. "Don't let the chickens eat the ladybugs. May I ask how I do that?" Shifting his attention to Chicken Soup seeming curious of Sugar's answer.

"I'll have my son teach you how to wrangle a huge chicken."

Store Number 1

Sugar Martin's Organic Food Store 1 fit like a glove inside the former Oldsmobile show room. Still rough looking and aged, the building served its purpose for Sugar. Garage doors opened up several times a day for Razzy driving in trucks of produce.

One garage door lifted up one morning, just light. In came a twelve foot long watermelon on a trailer. Had anyone ever seen a twelve foot watermelon?   Highly advertised, the oddity brought in a crowd.

The chainsaw made the first slice on the side, not the end. Customers waited in line for slices of watermelon, which they agreed tasted very sweet and crunchy. Sugar's idea of cutting up the melon inside and serving it to customers at the grand opening, on the first week of business, generated her motto.

Grow big, sell big.

Sugar Martin's Second Organic Food Store

Sugar followed the beam of Chris's flashlight to the old grocery store's office built onto the front wall. Now her office, her second store, Chris flipped the circuit breakers and the ceiling lights came to life. "Oh, my," Sugar said. The store was somewhat cleaned up by the previous store owners, they leaving behind a dirty smeared floor. Damaged tin cans left rings of rust on shelves. Dry cat food was scattered on the floor.

"There's a lot of work to do. Best get to it," she said.

Chris walked behind Sugar heading to the backroom. "Sugar, you're not doing the work, we have people for that, they will be here any minute."

She stopped and turned to him. "Working inside is a welcome change. There is a floor scrubber in the back, isn't there?"

"Yes." Chris said and answered his cell phone. "Chris Tatro. That's great." He snapped his phone shut. "Sugar, the logo is done."

"Oh, good." Sugar said stepping over a broken jar of pizza sauce, dried and molded, before going through the metallic swinging doors to the back workroom. She pulled out the floor machine and lifted the hood. It hit a garden hose curled up around water pipes and unrolled on the floor. She picked up the hose and dropped the nozzle into the water tank, and turned on the cold water. The water rose to a fill line inside the tank. She turned off the water, and pushed on a few knobs, not knowing how to run the machine. It appeared uncomplicated; it had to be like driving a riding mower.

The vacuum whooshed and the scrub pad whirred. Sugar pushed the machine effortlessly between the swinging doors, avoiding the broken glass, noting to clean it up when she found the proper equipment.

The machine made one clean path through the store to the front where dirty shoeprints tracked in at the entrance. As close to the storefront windows and doors as possible, Sugar maneuvered the machine inside the foyer.

Chris mapped out the produce bins for watermelon, cantaloupes, and strawberries. The apple table would be further away close to the front corner. Tomato shelving met the customer at the door, plus the extra bonus of the aroma of arousing onions and earthy potatoes.

His attention darted to two teenagers looking through the front glass doors. He waved them in. "You're here on time. Lonny and Bolynne? Uh, sorry, I don't remember who is who."

"I'm Bolynne Garey," the girl said.

"Lonny Malone, sir. We go to Marland High School. We signed up at the teen center for this job."

"Good, good, we have bins to build. Uh, come over here to the counter." Chris pulled manila folders out of his briefcase. "You understand how much you're being paid?" He thumped the papers. "I'm Chris Tatro, junior executive at Squarestone Enterprises." He gave Lonny and Bolynne each a folder. "Any questions?"

"None yet, sir, but if I think of any, I will ask," Lonny said.

Not expecting to be called sir, and not expecting him to be so polite and verbal, Chris replied, "Well, yes, I—I would expect you to ask. Uh, take these blueprints, and you'll find the lumber in the back rooms. You'll build the bins there."

38

The Lady in the Ladybug

Lonny held up the blueprints, pulled off his tape measure from a belt loop, and trotted to the metallic swinging door on the back wall. He measured the width of the door. "Won't fit through! We'll have to build them out on the floor." He peeked through the doors at the lumber.

Not expecting him to be so smart and inclined to figure, Chris sighed, rolling his eyes. Bolynne fluffed her long blonde hair, and took off for the backroom to be with Lonny. "Oh, boy," Chris whispered, moving out of the way of the scrubber.

Lonny put down the piece of lumber he carried. Bolynne did the same.

Sugar shut off the machine. "Hello!"

"Sugar, this is Lonny Malone and Bolynne Garey," Chris said.

They came towards Sugar and shook her hand.

"Who is who?"

"I'm Bolynne," she said, looking at Sugar's boots, and then at her fingers the way she pulled her floppy hat in place.

"And you must be Lonny," Sugar said, reaching for a handshake.

"Yes. I am so very pleased to meet you, Mrs. Martin."

"Oh, just call me Sugar. Well, best make the rounds," she said, flipping the switch on the scrubber.

"Please," Lonny interrupted her. "Let me do that."

"Why, what a thoughtful young man you are," she said, noticing Bolynne going to the other backroom, and Lonny pushing the floor machine from wall to wall.

Bolynne carried out more pieces of lumber and stacked them in a neat pile. Sugar stepped on the first step of short stairs up into the office. She tested it for strength, and then entered the room. Bolynne slightly smirked at Sugar's big butt the way it joggled when she climbed the four steps up into the office and came out with a broom and dustpan.

She swept up broken glass and dry cat food, and scraped the dried pizza sauce with her keys, and smiled at the floor becoming shiny clean. Chris hurried out of the backroom with four milk crates and placed boards on them. "Bolynne, have you ever used a hand saw?"

"No, but I've watched my father use one."

"Just place it on the mark, push and pull."

Bolynne took hold of the saw handle and settled the teeth on the mark. She pushed and pulled slowly, stopping and starting many times. Finally, after giving it all she had, she had command of it. The burr of the teeth grated a sound like *Sugar, Sugar, Sugar*. Bolynne looked up from sawing, turned around, and no one was speaking.

Lonny turned off the floor scrubber, and walked over to Bolynne, inspecting her work. She looked into his eyes and blushed, and continued sawing.

"Sugar, are we painting these bins?" Lonny asked.

"I think so," she said. "What color do you think is best?"

"Bolynne?" Lonny let her choose.

"Red."

"Really, that's my favorite color," Sugar said.

Bolynne added, "I like red because I like ladybugs."

Sugar cocked her head curiously. "That's a coincidence, so do I."

Three and Little, Inc.

Lee Three peered out his office window and saw two men and one woman wipe out dirt and organize loose papers in the government car abandoned yesterday in the parking lot of the convenience store. They pointed at the flat tire and examined the hood.

Three had a full view from two stories up showing the top of the car sliced, the hood scratched, and the trunk dented. He brainstormed how it got that way, and nothing came to mind.

The Lady in the Ladybug

The woman walked across the street to a clothing store, leaving the two men engaged in a conversation, rather heated. A bit of blaming seemed part of it since one had his finger in the other's face.

Glassburgh Tire Repair, a two-ton pickup with the name in red on the doors, parked near the car. A man spilled out with a tire iron, jacked up the back end, ripped off the flat, and then bounced out a new tire. He rolled the tire to the car and snapped it on like putting on a winter cap.

The woman returned to the car wearing a new pair of slacks. The two men got in the car, as did the woman, and they drove off.

Three broke from the window when someone knocked.

"Coming!" he hollered, almost at the door.

Three opened the wood door damaged by dripping water from an air conditioner unit above it.

Reva Little, dressed in designer clothing, new shoes, and well-manicured, carried a new attaché case, glanced over Three's musty cigarette smelling office and partial apartment that held boxes of bank statements, invoices, copies of receipts and dozens of receipts from renters. Coffee cans of pennies, nickels, dimes and quarters had been stacked in an open closet.

"Why don't you put that money in the bank?" She asked.

"I like having money around."

Reva nodded slightly and stared down at the crumb covered couch.

"Oh, here," he said, and raked the cushion off with his large hand.

"Thanks." She sat and looked up at the sagging ceiling. "Uh."

Three glanced up. "Hhm."

"You need a new office. You don't really live here, do you?"

"No, no. I have a real apartment over there a few blocks." He pointed lamely, and then scratched his head.

"Well, when you are rich, you can afford something a lot better." She eyed his black suit two sizes too large.

"You got a genie in that case?"

The Lady in the Ladybug

"I sure do, Three." She snapped open the case and handed to him a dozen papers. "I have a plan devised from simple human nature. This can change us into extremely successful. You see those early morning testimonies on television: make thousands weekly for following a plan. This is a plan for you, us, our partnership. Sell something everyone wants. Sell them an easy way of achieving what they want. We have what they want. Eating the locally grown food will cure diseases. Eating food grown in Sands County will prevent diseases. The world will come! It's so simple. They will believe it. Why? It's so unbelievably simple! The lavender haze is the reason. Sands County has the only lavender haze in the world. That's what makes the produce so healthy. We will even have the USDA stamp of approval." Reva showed a small photo from her attaché case. "Here is the proof. Bobby Click. Native of Glassburgh, left town after high school, worked various places in Texas, Missouri, and Florida. Drank a little too much. Got a doctor's report that if he quit drinking, ate good healthy food, he'd return to normal health. Now he's back in Glassburgh. He's going to work for your new produce store."

Three shook his head. "I can see lawsuits."

"Won't happen."

"Now that's something you see on television all the time. Call me, Joe Smith, didn't get your health back after eating Lee Three's produce?"

"How many people have sued those body shaping weight loss programs?"

"Wouldn't know."

"No one. No one wants to have that out in the public."

Three sat. He stared at the floor. "Don't see how it's the same."

"Is that a balcony?" Reva asked.

"Yep."

Reva stepped around boxes of paperwork and bank statements, and pushed curtains away from the door. The wood screen door

42

opened, hinges creaking, scaring pigeons away. She looked down at the street. A tow truck parked in the convenience store lot. The driver exited it and looked puzzled as to why the car he was told to tow was gone.

Giant Chicken

Dix pulled into the garage, took out the keys, and tossed them to the mechanic on duty who frowned, curled his lip at looking upon the slices and dents. "How did this happen?"

"Uh, you know, rough country out around where we inspected." Dix smirked, proud of his answer. He strutted out of the garage, and into the elevator.

Mal marched to Director Luke Welch's office and knocked with urgency.

"Come in, Fordors. The soil samples, how many did you collect?"

"Funny you asked, Sir. You see, we had an accident."

Welch squinted. "Car accident?"

"Yes, in a way. A giant chicken attacked the car."

Welch put down his pen and leered at Mal. "When I hired you I was a little hesitant, now I know why."

"But I have witnesses, Dix and Jo."

Welch pushed a button on the phone, and commanded Jo and Dix to come into the office. He mumbled and laughed. "Giant chicken." He waited, watching the clock, staring at Mal, and slyly smiled.

Mal looked up at the ceiling at the security camera. A ladybug flew past and landed on the desk. Welch looked at it, and watched Mal watching it walk across the desk. Taking mental notes of each step, and when it took flight, Mal noticed the outer shell. It rose, and then

The Lady in the Ladybug

gray wings spread out for takeoff, and that's all he could see before it buzzed away.

The door opened. Dix and Jo stepped in, saw Mal biting his lip, and gave their undivided attention to Welch. He pointed. "Sit."

"I don't know what he's telling you, but it's all true," Dix said.

"Jo?" Welch asked her.

"Every ounce of it, all true," she said.

Welch pressed a button on the phone. "We'll have someone else go to Glassburgh." He garbled out some orders and chuckled, keeping an eye on Mal, Dix, and Jo. That phone call ended, and a collective sigh from the three hoping they were off the hook until the phone rang, Welch's eyes grew shiny in anger, and he blurted, "The car is what?" He sputtered to the mechanic restating, "Dented and sliced." Welch dismissed the mechanic on the phone, and glared. "A simple assignment," he grumbled to the trio, "I get a wild story and destroyed government property. Answer me that riddle." He zeroed in on Dix. "Let's start with you, Mr. Caddo."

He smiled lazily. "The giant chicken, sir, we were walking back to the car after the ladybug ride, and when I turned the key, the car wouldn't start. So we logically looked under the hood, and didn't learn anything. Mal volunteered to walk to the nearest house and ask for help. He had gone about a four yards and looked up at this huge, giant chicken snorting and pawing the ground meaning to attack him, so he ran back to the car. The chicken attacked us in the car, and we decided to run to the trees and climb them to get away from it."

Welch stared at Dix. "You said a ladybug ride?" He looked around for the ladybug that was just landed on his desk.

"Yes, Sugar Martin has a huge ladybug—"

"Mrs. Harris, what's your side of this story?" Welch asked.

"It's true. On Sugar Martin's farm, she has a giant ladybug that she rides, and a huge pet chicken that is sort of mean. It chased us up a tree that was really an enormous asparagus plant."

44

"And don't forget the lavender haze," Mal spurted.

Welch held up his hand, he didn't want to hear anymore. "Be back here Monday, on time, and during that time, get some sleep."

"Thank you, sir," Jo said.

"There's Trouble in the Watermelon."

The first customer to enter Sugar Martin's Organic Store 2 pulled a shopping cart out of the nest. Business people from downtown came in, and presented Sugar with a flower arrangement, and wished her the best. Mylar balloons floated above with congratulations printed on them.

"Wishing you success, Sugar," a man in a business suit said, taking her hand and shaking it, heartily.

"Thank you!" Dressed in her usual polka dot dress, rubber boots, and floppy hat, some customers looked her over, wanting to know if it were a gimmick to dress like that. Some whispered the dress had been worn some, so, not a new thing, or was it?

"Roxy! Roxy!" A woman pushing a loaded cart caught up with Sugar.

"Rosa!"

"La tienda es buena."

"Thank you, how are you?" She patted her shoulder.

"Bien. Your son is well?"

"Oh, yes."

"Casado?"

"No. He is still single."

"Your family?"

"Oh," Rosa turned sad. "My niece, she has breast cancer."

"I'm so sorry. How old is she?" Sugar asked, her hand over her heart.

"Only thirty, has a little girl of her own." A slight smile emerged.

The Lady in the Ladybug

Sugar shook her head in sympathy. Seeing another customer approaching her, Rosa went on to the onions and potatoes.

Sugar wished Rosa a good day, savoring the moment of friendship she had with her, whom she had been since childhood.

A tall skinny man wearing a suit coat too large pushed an empty cart past. He looked curiously at her, as if wanting to ask a question. His beaky nose and thin face made him more alike a bird, a buzzard circling prey.

"Finding everything you need?" Sugar asked.

He nodded, and went on his way about the store. Sugar gathered around women laughing about the silly squash.

"Twist it, bend it, it won't ever break," she explained.

"But how does it taste?" asked Jackie, a small woman wearing purple scrubs.

"Like very good sweet squash. It is so moist inside, but not mushy, the skin of these squash is part rubber." Sugar explained, wide-eyed.

"Where do they come from?" Jackie asked.

"My organic farm, I invented it." Sugar explained, turning the squash over and over.

"Isn't rubber man made?" Another woman asked.

"No," Sugar retorted. "You have heard of a rubber tree? They originally grew in Africa. I flew over there to get one."

"How exotic," they echoed.

"Just cook it in its skin, let cool, squeeze out like toothpaste. Silly as that!" Sugar laughed, and slowly walked away.

❖

Store 1 had a situation. Sugar listened to her employee explain, sniffling at what the man tried to do.

"In the watermelon? You are kidding me. Did you call the police? Really? Not doing anything wrong."

The Lady in the Ladybug

Sugar flipped her phone shut. Sugar Martin Organic Store 1 had attracted the curious. Her gigantic watermelon just had a visitor.

"Razzy! There's trouble in the watermelon! Follow me to the store on Gossamer Avenue."

Razzy grinned, "I got to see this."

"See what?" asked Bobby.

"She was the county wrestling champ when she was twenty-something."

"This I got to see." Bobby hurried to his pickup. Razzy hopped in, pulling the door shut, leaning out the window. "There!" He pointed, and Bobby sped up to twenty miles an hour just underneath Cleopatra. Bobby honked the horn.

Razzy laughed.

Bobby looked over at Razzy. "I want them to know we're down here."

"We need to take you on a ride. All you can hear is wings and the wind," Razzy said.

"That's quite all right," Bobby said. "How do you keep from falling out?" Bobby asked, flashing his eyes from the road to the sky.

"Her inner wing holds you in place. You do need a ride," Razzy said.

Bobby stopped for the red light "Has anyone ever noticed?"

"Most people think she's man made," he said. "There, over there is where she'll land."

They saw her landing on a baseball field with bleachers and a concession stand. Marland High School set across the street near the tower. It had crisscross steel supports about three feet apart. It reached up into the sky higher than the tower of Babylon. He pointed at it, looking intently at Razzy. "Did you climb that?"

"I did several times, made it to the top."

"And you?"

"Uh-uh," he moaned and stopped the pickup.

The Lady in the Ladybug

A slipper slide and seesaw near the bleachers entertained a couple of boys. Their attention went up to the sky. They pointed at Cleopatra and watched her land. Sugar slipped out.

Bobby and Razzy leapt out of the pickup and stood by Cleopatra, frozen into place. The boys walked around it, feeling the shell, and stood on her head to climb up onto the top of the ladybug, but it proved too slippery. Razzy crowded them out, protecting Cleopatra's eyes.

"What's it made out of?" the smaller boy asked.

"Plastic," Razzy answered.

"Isn't there a pilot inside?" The older boy asked, peering in the eye.

"Uh, no, it's remote controlled."

"Where's the remote?"

Razzy pointed. "Up in that tower!" He waved as if he was signaling someone.

"Make it fly."

He tried to come up with an answer. "Wave up at the top." They looked up at Razzy, squinting and thinking hard about the tower and possibly it had this special equipment and they never knew. They turned their heads gazing up at the point of the tower.

Razzy and Bobby left the boys puzzled, and crossed the street. A half block ahead, they spotted Sugar hurrying around people. A few recognized the floppy hat, the polka dot dress with rubber boots. She stopped at the check stands, bent over, caught her breath a bit, and after composing herself, she clomped toward the watermelon, sounding ominous, foreboding.

She popped inside, asking why he hid in the watermelon, and why he didn't leave when the staff asked him.

He only ignored Sugar.

She folded her arms, looked him over, kind of dirty. "Mister, I am asking you to please leave the watermelon. You cannot stay here much longer; we will close the store at eight sharp." He lifted his eyebrows, he understood, but didn't care. Sugar planted her feet in front of him, almost stepping on a plastic bag. She could see a flannel shirt in the bag and maybe another pair of Levis. A leather belt and red bandana swirled around the clothing.

Sympathy for the man became greater than fear of him or the necessity to rid him of her store.

"Okay, I see you don't have a place to stay the night, so I am going to put you up in a motel. If you will follow me."

He stared straight ahead, motionless. Sugar looked back at him. "Did you hear me? A motel? Of your choice!" He ignored her, smirking. She wrapped her hands around his upper arms, and lifted him off the watermelon floor. He grabbed his sack before Sugar heisted him above her head. He cursed and growled on his way out of the watermelon. Sugar walked past the staff with hands over snickering mouths. Customers dropped their mouths open at the sight of a grown man carried out by a large woman in a polka dot dress. She spun in a circle for ten seconds then let the stranger down, and he stumbled off, running a crooked line.

The employees applauded. Bobby laughed hard. Razzy grinned, "That's my mother."

Lonny and Bolynne

Never a dull moment in her stores, especially Store 2 on Turnage Street when Chris came up with to Sugar, announcing…

"A television cooking show featuring you as hostess. Broadcast—" Chris' arms went way above his head, "To the entire state."

"Me as the hostess?" Sugar asked, eyes brightening in anger. "We just opened another grocery store; I have to spend a lot of time here."

"Sugar, we'll film it here, we'll build a kitchen — the possibilities!" His hands again pounced up like he was about to throw a basket.

"Too much work." She said shaking her head.

"I have committed the corporation to it. They want a cookbook, and a line of food." Now his hands were on his hips.

"Chris, it is *toooooo* time consuming! I have my organic farm and two stores." She stared him down, not letting him get his way.

"I signed a contract."

Sugar didn't react. She only pointed. "Get them to do the show, they're good young people, look how charming they are as a couple. Good workers. I bet they would <u>love</u> the opportunity. Go ask them."

Chris pouted as he watched Lonny and Bolynne pick up items to purchase. He noticed their genuine smiles at the people they met in the store.

"Lonny," Chris called. "Have time for another job?"

"Hey, Chris, how are you?" He shook his hand.

"Sugar recommended you for this." He wrapped his arms around Lonny and Bolynne's shoulders. "She thinks you two would be great for a cooking show we are filming here in the store, uh, right over there." Chris pointed both hands at the spice racks. Lonny and Bolynne briefly looked at the racks of spices imported from an organic supplier with a foreign name.

 "We'll build a kitchen there — put in a sink, fridge, oven, all brand shiny new. Want to read the contract?" Chris asked, handing his phone to Lonny.

"Uh, can I have my dad look it over?" Lonny said without taking it from him.

"Sure, Bolynne?"

"I'm going to be on television? Every week?"

"Yes."

"I'll sign now."

The Lady in the Ladybug

"Bolynne, not too quick. Let's read it first," Lonny warned.

"Read, read, and today. The corporation is anxious. What's your dad's email?"

Atla Flowers, secretary, bookkeeper, assistant store manager, and CFO turned in the previous day's total income to Sugar. Very good, Sugar noted on the paper. All her hard work was supporting so many people. Razzy was doing what he loved, and so was she. Atla laid down an envelope from the USDA. Sugar sliced it open. She had been approved.

"I knew they would," she said cheerfully.

"Did I hear right? A cooking show here in the store?" Atla asked.

Sugar frowned. "I'm not in it. I refused."

"Why?" Atla asked seriously.

"Me on television? Have you not seen how large I am?" Sugar glanced over the top of the computer monitor and down at Chris talking to Lonny and Bolynne. Lonny read from his phone and Bolynne laughed and flirtingly pretended to be stirring something. She fed Chris a spoonful of the imaginary food.

"He is holding auditions down there," Sugar told Atla.

"Uh-huh," she said, peeking down.

Chris popped into the office. "Sugar, Bolynne had a great idea. You appear in the beginning of each show and then reappear at the end, to eat what is cooked."

"I'll taste what is cooked."

"Yes, the audience will want you to <u>taste</u> what is prepared, Sugar. The audience wants complete trust that you eat the silly squash, the curly squash, and the lavender beets."

Sugar ignored Chris and glanced out the office window. That man was pushing an empty cart over the entire store, without purchasing one item. She pointed at the man for Atla to identify.

She recognized him with a smile. "That's Lee Three."

"What does he do beside push an empty grocery cart around my store?"

"He owns a lot of buildings and properties in Glassburgh. Sometimes he thinks he owns the town. But if I had as many investments as he does, I'd be cautious about what goes on."

"I can understand that," replied Sugar. But she didn't understand. Why wasn't he watching his own buildings and properties?

That Someone Else goes to Glassburgh

Farina Moss walked into the store ready for her six hours at the apple station. She entered the break room and placed her purse in her locker. Clocking in on time, she put on her name badge and public personality and went for the apple station. It was a wooden desk with a lip around the top to prevent apples from rolling onto the floor.

The top drawer possessed the shining cloth that Atla presented to her yesterday at the short training session. Atla's black piercing eyes with severe black eyebrows dipped over her eyes when she gave the orders about money, customer service, and equipment. What she said about the cloth rang in her ears, 'Don't lose them. Keep them in your drawer, locked, when not using one.' Farina nodded, following the orders. She recalled the ledger kept in the third drawer, and Atla opening it, pointing at the left column with her long red fingernail. "Write in how many boxes of apples you sell at the end of your shift." Her long red dagger pressed on the right column. "Write down the impulse items you display, peanut butter, caramel, or honey. Down those two diagonal aisles are the only grocery supplies. Dust those off, face up the products; stock them from the back stock in the backroom."

The Lady in the Ladybug

Atla peeked at her through the office window. Farina didn't know why, she was there and there on time, but two men in black suits appeared to Farina and asked if Sugar was in the store.

"Atla would know." She pointed at the window.

One of the men handed her a few colorful pamphlets. "We're handing these out to promote the tree festival in August. We usually give each station a few."

"Okay," she said, reading the front cover and flipping to the back, putting one in her back pocket.

She focused in on her work observing how the red, yellow, and green apples were stacked neatly inside baskets. Fresh from the organic orchard, the apples were mixed together, not displayed separately, as the major supermarkets sold fruit. For the hand of a fussy shopper, apples filled half full inside the basket.

She heard a truck bellow at the dock of the store through the metallic swinging doors. Voices grew louder, but no distinct words, just voices. Happy voices though. A man brought out a big box of apples and set them on the floor beside the station. He said hello to her; she said hello in return. They looked at each other for a moment, eyes locking, lingering. Farina smiled and extended her hand.

"Farina."

"Razzy Martin. Sugar is my mother."

"I haven't met her yet."

"You will." He regarded her as he turned away. Built of muscles, he looked as if he had worked hard all his life. Tanned and rugged, slight wrinkles around his eyes, and his clothing was for hard work, patched and frayed. He looked back at her before he disappeared behind the swinging doors. Farina waved at him, and then proceeded to shine the red apples with the special cloth. It felt heavy and measured a little less than a handkerchief. Moist, a spongy texture, and it had the strangest characteristic of tiny circles attached together. She placed it over an apple on the desk and the cloth contoured itself around the apple.

53

The Lady in the Ladybug

She heard someone behind her. Someone huge and heavy breathing warm air down on top her head. Farina tried not to act perturbed, yet, she spun around and became face to bosom with a large woman looking down at her, sporting a little smile, lifting her large hand to greet.

"Sugar Martin and you are Farina?"

"Yes, Farina Moss." She backed up a bit.

Sugar picked up the treasured shining cloth and held it on both hands. "Guard these. I spent many years, many experiments developing them. We don't wax apples like the supermarkets, I organically shine them." She rubbed the cloth between her hands. "As you will see, how my hands warm the cloth." She placed it over the apple on the desk, and rubbed the apple in a washing motion. After the shining cloth was removed, the apple shined brighter than a new car.

Farina picked the apple up and looked at it closely. Amazing how that cloth changed the apple peeling's appearance.

Chris called for Sugar. She turned, acknowledged him, and excused herself.

"Sure," Farina said. Her phone rang; she pulled it out of her trouser pocket and turned off the ringer.

"Fresh apples from the orchard?"

"Yes, they are. Hello Mr. Three. Thanks for renting me an apartment."

She found it strange that he was in this store, when he told her he had a store similar to this one.

He glanced around, scrutinizing things. "Where'd you say you were from?"

"San Amez."

A noise from the television show's set took their attention. Sugar listened to Chris talking while the crew hung wire for the television stage lights.

Three took two green apples and went towards Sugar.

The Lady in the Ladybug

Farina watched a young couple join Sugar and Three. They laughed when Chris told them something. The girl with cutoffs, tank top, and flip-flops, spoke with everyone attentively listening. The boy wearing nice slacks and shirt put some actions and sound effects into the story, and they laughed harder. Chris handed a book to the girl. She looked at the cover and raised her eyebrows at her companion. She pressed her finger on the photo on the cover and flipped open the book, showing him.

Razzy plopped down another box of apples. Farina smiled and thanked him. He walked away but found his way back to Farina.

"How would you like a grand tour of the farm? Tonight at six okay? I'll pick you up. Mom loves guests for dinner."

"Oh, I would," Farina said, sincerely. She stared into Razzy's eyes.

"Good. Pick you up — where do you live?"

"Lee Three Apartments across the street — that way. I'll be ready." Farina watched Razzy leave.

Chris hauled out the final shelf out of the spice corner. He walked past Razzy nearing the swinging doors and said hello, then disappeared into the back room. He returned with two chairs and an empty box as a desk.

The young couple sat and throughout the cookbook they circled recipes they liked. Chris had a small box of vegetables for them to take home and practice cutting like the chefs on television. "Don't cut your fingers off," he said. "Bolynne, have you found a recipe? Pineapple Upside Cake is always a favorite."

Bolynne frowned and looked at Lonny and then at Chris. "What if what we bake doesn't turn out well? When we take it out of the oven, it's a flop? We need to have a finished cake to display when we are done."

"How much time have you spent in the kitchen, Bolynne?" Chris asked her.

Not much. Too many school activities."

"I see. Well, I guess I could bake these cakes …" Chris thought, and turned around. "Hmm," he hummed. He took off toward Farina. She saw him coming toward her with a determined smile. It also appeared he was decided when he commented that she looked like a cook.

"I love to cook, why?"

Chris motioned at Bolynne and Lonny to come over. "You see, we're doing a cooking show in the store, and our chefs aren't too experienced. I wanted Sugar to host the show but she declined. We need someone to bake the finished product. One that will look great on camera."

Farina smiled anticipating his next question.

"Have you met Lonny Malone and Bolynne Garey?"

"No, hello — I'm Farina Moss."

"Glad to meet you, Miss Moss," Lonny said.

Bolynne shook her hand.

"How about we get together tonight?" Chris asked.

"Uh, I have another invitation."

Chris nodded, looking toward the office window. "I think Sugar would like to know you are working with the show."

"I'll tell her tonight when I am at the farm."

"Doing what?" He asked, surprised.

"I was invited by Razzy. Anything else you want to know?"

"No, no," he said. He looked away.

"I'll be here tomorrow, call or come by and we'll work out a time," Farina said.

"Great, I'll be looking forward to that."

Lonny and Bolynne politely excused themselves as the carpenter dragged a ladder and set it up.

Another man wheeled in boxes with the words stage lights on the sides. He had a cordless drill and a level.

Atla handed her an apple.

The Lady in the Ladybug

"No charge. Sugar wants all the new employees to taste the merchandise. Enjoy," Atla said.

Farina rubbed the apple on her shirt sleeve ready to take a bite when an employee walked past the activity at the television set and stopped in front of the apple station. "I'm relieving you for lunch," Colette told Farina.

"Any good places you recommend for lunch? Close by?"

"Try Ricky's a couple blocks north of the park. Very good."

"Which park?"

Colette whined, "The park over there."

Farina showed thumbs up and assumed it was very close, so out the door she went, walked around the store, and could see a grassy area with some equipment. Brick streets surrounded the park.

The first store on the end of the block was an antique store, a printing business, and then Ricky's. The buildings were old, and were maintained to look old. Casement windows, old doors, and wood floors in Ricky's had that European feel. Ricky himself welcomed her and suggested either the salad bar or the hot bar.

"Hmm," Farina said. "Better take the salad bar. I'm invited out to dinner tonight, so better go light for lunch."

Ricky agreed, and set down a glass of water at the booth she chose. He escorted her to the salad bar and told her it was all she could eat, or wanted to eat. Farina thanked him. She filled a bowl, thinking about Razzy, about Sugar, and what she would see at the farm. That had her very curious.

Ricky walked past. "Do you need more water? Anything else I can get you?"

"No. I'm fine. But you can tell me about Glassburgh. What's the thing that draws people here?"

Ricky smiled. "People here are the healthiest in the world. That has been studied over the past fifty years. It is attributed to clean air and water, organic food and something scientists can't understand."

The Lady in the Ladybug

"It wouldn't be the lavender haze, would it? Or the asteroid hit? I have lived in San Amez all my life. I've only been in Glassburgh a few times."

Ricky nodded. "Glassburgh wasn't popular until the past few years. When a healthier lifestyle was promoted, the businesses decided they were sitting on a goldmine."

Farina pointed her finger at her head. "That is smart thinking. So do people live long lives?"

"You bet. We have several one hundred year olds living in their own homes."

Farina opened her mouth in awe. "Really."

"Yep."

"So you think the town is growing?"

"I see new faces every week."

Someone called for Ricky and he excused himself to the kitchen.

Farina munched down the last piece of broccoli, put down money on the ticket, and departed Ricky's.

Those two Glassburgh skyscrapers burst their prisms of light into the sky. In the noon sun, every inch of the rooms was brightened. Wasn't it hot inside? She met a man in a business suit going into Ricky's. She flagged him down, "Aren't the skyscrapers hot inside? Being made of glass?"

"Engineered to catch the heat for water and power for electricity."

"That makes sense."

She looked in the antique store windows and browsed the displays. Propped up against a decorative box was a souvenir plate with one of the San Amez skiing resorts painted on it and next to it was another plate with the Glassburgh skyscrapers. She bet more people went to San Amez on vacation than to Glassburgh. San Amez had the industries for people to work, not Glassburgh.

San Amez was spread out within those mountains; Glassburgh was flat.

The Lady in the Ladybug

San Amez was the capitol and had all the federal offices. San Amez had frivolous businesses; Glassburgh had practical businesses. No hat shops in Glassburgh. Nothing exciting in Glassburgh.

She walked across the street. A few children were in the park with their mothers. Farina smiled, hoping she would be a mother one day and with her children in a park, but not in Glassburgh, in San Amez. Meeting anyone compatible in San Amez was a full-time avocation. Church, sports events, and hanging around in men's clothing stores she had all tried. Bombed out all the time.

Back inside the store, the aroma of cantaloupe filled the air. Those cantaloupes were the size of watermelons, normal watermelons. In line to buy one were several people. She attended her apple table and filled several orders. She filled customers' requests while they shopped. By two o'clock, she took two trips to the back room to stock the table, counted the boxes, and wrote in the ledger. Her relief arrived on time and introduced herself, Florence.

Farina checked her cell phone messages on the way out the door. Two from Luke Welch. He told her to call him in the first message, and the second, he told her to call him now.

Farina at the Farm

"Hey, sis, no, I'm in Glassburgh, yes, well, I'm finding out. I don't know how long I'll be here, hopefully only a few days." She kicked off her shoes, "Oh, the view from my balcony is wonderful. The glass skyscraper is beautiful when the sun shines on it." She reached for an outfit out of her suitcase. "Top secret? No, just following up on the previous inspectors' reports that the boss couldn't accept. Strange things. Hey, I've got to jump in the shower. I'll call you tomorrow. Bye, love you."

The Lady in the Ladybug

Farina sat on the bench outside the apartment complex and checked her phone for the third time, and Razzy drove up. He hopped out of the average looking and not so new pickup. He smiled on his way to the bench. "Hello, hope you're hungry, mom is cooking up a storm." He extended his arm for her to hold onto, and she sensed his hard as stone bicep.

His pickup sported a new magnetic sign on the door, and the closer she came to it, she could see the letters and details. *Sugar Martin Organic Food Stores* in purple letters over rows and rows of green crops, and Sugar standing in the field wearing her trademark floppy hat, a white and orange polka dot dress, and rubber boots.

Razzy opened the door for her and helped her in the truck. He checked that she climbed in properly and shut the door. He walked behind his truck and plopped on the seat where he had worn a spot.

"You've lived here all your life, Razzy?"

"Yes."

"Do you have any other siblings?"

"No, just me. How about you?" He turned onto a road that led out of town.

"One sister, one brother."

A curvy road went uphill; the tops of trees tickled the side of the road. He slowed down and turned on a road that deepened to the floor of the forest. That road led to a crossroads and he kept going straight. Thick trees thinned and more land bared itself.

Green farm equipment dotted the earth. The plowed dark lavender fields reached up to the setting sun and fields extended and stretched for miles and miles into infinite rows.

"How long are these fields?" Farina asked.

"Some days they are too long. It seems I never get done."

"I'm sure. Don't you have farm hands?"

"During the harvest."

"How many acres?"

"Sounds like you are doing a report." He looked at her for a definite answer.

"No, I'm just interested. I'm curious at heart."

A white house poked out above a green field. Climbing roses covered most of the fences; flowers bloomed in beds on the side of the house. The scent of them overpowered when she stepped out of the pickup.

"Achew." Farina excused herself, and followed Razzy along the path that changed into a cement walk to the front door.

Sugar stood in the doorway, sporting a large smile, and holding a wooden spatula. She took Farina's hand and heartily shook it; Farina felt grease on Sugar's fingers. An aroma of coffee, fruit and something saucy cooked in the kitchen thirty feet from the front door. Farina noticed the kitchen to be quite modern and update. Shiny and clean, Sugar had everything put in its place and within reach on the countertop, an island that curved with a little sink on the end.

"Farina, have a seat here. You've worked hard all day," Sugar said, patting a chair.

"I wouldn't mind sitting."

Razzy helped his mother set the table and replenish a vase with fresh flowers. Farina squinted at them. "What do you call that color?"

"Of?" Sugar asked.

"The flowers."

"It's called leck," Sugar said. She plopped the bowl of meatballs and pasta on the table, and popped a lid off the salad crunchies over the lettuce. She sprinkled them generously. Farina stared at the tricolor lettuce; red, blue, and leck.

"Leck is only a color found in the plant world," Sugar said. "It can't be reproduced on fabric or paint."

"Really," said Farina. "That is fascinating."

"Shall we eat?" Sugar asked.

"Yes, I'm starving," Razzy said. He pulled out a chair for his mother. Though Sugar remained standing and scooped a serving of pasta onto a plate and handed it to Farina. She served Razzy's plate a bit heavier, and then Sugar plopped down a ladle of pasta and about five meatballs for herself.

"So, how long has your family been farming here? Your ancestors came from where? Germany?" Farina asked.

Sugar glanced at Razzy. "Well, we didn't come from anywhere. We have been here since — since we can remember."

"Oh, since childhood, then—"

"Yes, but you don't understand. We didn't come from anywhere."

"Where were you born?" Farina asked.

"Right here in this house," Sugar said.

Farina frowned, and looked at her food, and picked up her fork. She ate quickly. Razzy watched her, a little intrigued. He stuffed an entire meatball into his mouth. Sugar nibbled on a meatball, and when she had it a manageable size, she popped it in.

Sugar passed the pasta and meatballs, and offered more water. She laughed a bit. "My mother would always make fun of the dramas on television when the actresses ate. 'Oh, they just ate and their lipstick didn't come off.'"

Farina chuckled, dabbing her mouth with the napkin.

"Are we ready for dessert?" Sugar asked.

"You bet," Razzy said, anticipating.

Sugar took a spatula to the dessert cooling on a countertop. She stuck the utensil in and pried a piece of raspberry malt cake with chocolate topping out onto a small plate. With three plates filled and returned to the table, Sugar waited for their reaction.

Farina took one taste, swallowed the bite, and raised one finger. "Uh?"

Sugar frowned, stabbing a piece over and over.

Razzy took a double take at the window. Chicken Soup walked past, back and forth, peeking inside.

The Lady in the Ladybug

"Look, we don't have to eat it — I have ice cream in the freezer." Sugar searched Razzy's and Farina's faces.

Razzy jumped up and ran outside. Farina followed him.

"No, no, no," Sugar cried. "The dessert is terrible."

She heard Razzy yell.

"OH! NO!" Sugar ran out of the house. Razzy wrangled Chicken Soup and Farina stood by, not smiling, not frowning, but only staring in disbelief.

Razzy climbed up Chicken Soup's leg, grabbing hold of feathers, and sat on her back and commanded her to go to the barn on the other side of the house. Sugar and Farina ran over to it, and watched Razzy trick Chicken Soup into the barn. He slid off, tumbled on the ground, and picked himself up, running through the door that Sugar held open wide enough for only him. She slammed the door shut.

Chicken Soup angrily pecked the barn door.

Farina stood in a daze while Razzy dusted himself off. Sugar wiped her hands on her apron.

"Well, dessert is waiting for us," Sugar said, smiling.

"Let's go," Razzy said. He gave his mother the right of way with a sweeping arm, and asked Farina to go ahead of him.

Sugar lumbered in front of Farina. She taking two steps to Sugar's one.

Razzy opened the door for them. They sat at the table and settled in to finish the dessert. Farina picked at the dessert, thinking, pondering, and scrutinizing. The lavender haze, a giant chicken and somewhere hid a huge ladybug that Sugar used for transportation, according to the other agents. A very strange place, yet the air smelled so pure and fertile. It was the first time she had breathed rich farm soil. She had smelled outdoors for the first time. What she liked most was that she liked this place.

"Explain what you said, you have always been here."

Sugar nodded. "My lineage goes back to right here. We have lived on this piece of land for thousands of years."

Farina listened. "That's fascinating. Tell me more."

"The outside world never bothered. We kept to ourselves."

"It's getting late, Farina. Are you ready to go to your apartment?" Razzy asked.

"Oh, sure. Let's go." She stood and shook Sugar's hand.

He held the front door open for her. "Your family history must be truly interesting," Farina said. Sugar picked out a meatball and popped it into her mouth, listening. "The stories you must have to tell," Farina said.

Sugar looked a little confused.

"It's colorful. Never a dull moment around here," said Razzy on the way outside.

Sugar watched them walk out. She tried to sum her up. *Seems she was trying to find out something.*

The Television Cooking Show

Peppy music played while Chubb, the cameraman, panned Sugar Martin's Organic Store 2. He focused on the silly squash and the tricolor lettuce. That faded into the television set where Sugar stood in front of the counter, holding a large stalk of asparagus. Chubb pointed at the red light on the camera and Sugar's wide-eyed stare at him put a grin on the middle-aged part Cherokee cameraman.

"Welcome," she waved the asparagus across her chest, "To Sugar Martin's Cooking Show with our hosts Lonny Garey, no, uh, I mean—Lonny Malone and Bolynne Garey."

Lonny and Bolynne paused a second, swallowing hard, and forcing a smile.

The Lady in the Ladybug

"Hello, Bolynne, hello, Lonny," Sugar said in a monotone stage fright voice. "What are you cooking today?"

"A peach cobbler with homemade ice cream." Chubb pointed at his ear. Bolynne raised her eyebrows, and talked louder. "LONNY HAS SET OUT ALL THE INGREDIENTS."

Chubb waved her down a bit. She nodded, her mouth wide open.

"I'll be anticipating this wonderful dessert," said Sugar, dashing out of the camera's view.

The red light disappeared, and a commercial played from local businesses. Lonny and Bolynne nervously watched the digital clock on the television screen near the camera. Shoppers watched the cooking show from their shopping carts jamming the aisles. Some shoppers pushed through the congestion and didn't pay attention to the show. Chubb pointed at the red light, and panned the camera over the glass measuring dishes filled with flour, sugar, and milk, and cream.

"I have premeasured the cream, vanilla, sugar," Lonny said. "We blend those ingredients and then pour them in the freezer. I'll turn it on and let it churn. Now the cobbler, Bolynne."

Reading off her script on the counter, Bolynne slowly read the recipe. "One and one half cups flour, one and one fourth cups sugar, one and one half teaspoon baking powder and one cup milk." She looked up at the camera, and then at Lonny mixing the ingredients. "Lonny is mixing all this together. I have melted one stick of butter into a thirteen by nine inch glass-baking dish in the oven." Her shaking hands slid into baking mitts and she set the hot baking dish on the counter.

Lonny turned to Bolynne, "I'll pour in the mixed ingredients."

Chubb took a close up of the batter.

"Pour the two and one half cups peaches in juice on top the mixture. You will have to separate the peach slices by moving them apart with a utensil. In this bowl," Lonny held up, "Is one cup sugar mixed with one fourth teaspoon of cinnamon. Sprinkle that over the peaches. Bake at three hundred fifty degrees for thirty to forty minutes."

"The oven is ready," Bolynne said. "We preheated it to 523."

Lonny turned his head toward her and winked. "Three hundred twenty five degrees."

She opened the oven and placed the baking dish inside. "Yes, that's what I said. While we are waiting for the ice cream and cobbler, Lonny and I visited Sugar Martin's organic farm and toured the orchard."

Lonny and Bolynne faded on screen and trees in the orchard appeared. They walked through the orchard with Sugar and Razzy.

Farina put on oven mitts and took the peach cobbler she had baked earlier out of the warmer. She placed it on the countertop with dessert plates and spoons. Sugar tiptoed up to the counter, waiting for Chubb's cue to finish the show.

Razzy lightly walked over to Chubb, and stood beside him, trying to catch Farina's attention. She looked up and smiled at seeing him, and snuck away from the set.

Chubb counted down the video, and pointed at Lonny. "It," Lonny said and paused, seeing Chubb move in for a close-up. Lonny stuck a wooden spatula into a corner and delivered a small sampling onto a dessert plate. "It smells great," he said to Bolynne, adding a scoop of ice cream.

"It smells so good, I'd eat the whole thing, but of course, I'd wouldn't," Bolynne giggled, winking into the camera. She handed the first serving to Sugar.

She took a bite and smiled as she swallowed. "Mmm, wonderful, this is such a good cobbler recipe and it baked so well."

"Bolynne," Lonny said, "It's time to treat the shoppers."

She set plates of dessert on a cart to wheel to the customers. Chubb followed; shoppers smiled hesitantly, some waved enthusiastically into the camera lens.

The Lady in the Ladybug

When Farina broadcast over the store that they shared the dessert with the customers, shoppers whizzed to the corner.

Chubb closed in on Sugar. "Tomorrow," she said, "We will slice up fresh pineapple, and have Pineapple Upside Down Cake served with homemade topping. See you tomorrow." Chubb panned the store and shoppers for fifteen seconds until he ended the show.

They took a break for an hour or more, until the filming of the second show.

Five, four, three, two, one … Chubb said, pointing at the red light. Sugar read from the computer screen near the camera operator. "Our recipe for Pineapple Upside Down cake with cherries is simple. We'll show you in a minute, but first, today is the judging of the trees. Entrants are anxiously awaiting that visit from the award's committee with a winner's ribbon. We have film of past winners, and their story."

The segment played while Bolynne and Lonny took one more look at the ingredients, making sure they had everything for the cake. Lonny took the cue, and sliced the pineapple meat. Bolynne watched for a couple seconds. "Very nice slices, Lonny."

"Thank you, Bolynne. We have prepared cake batter and brown sugar, pineapple slices, and cherries. First, though, we melt a stick of butter, real organic butter, in the cake pan, it can be glass or metal, arrange the pineapple rings with a cherry in each circle, crumble the cup and a half of brown sugar on top that, and pour in the prepared cake batter. Put in the preheated oven for twenty-five minutes at three hundred twenty five degrees, and wait for a very good dessert."

"It's that simple, Lonny, as we already know, since we have a cake baked." Bolynne opened the oven. She shot a terrified look at Lonny and slapped her hands over her mouth. Sugar came into view with the baked Pineapple Upside Down Cake with candles lit.

"Happy Birthday, Bolynne," Sugar said, setting down the cake. "Make a wish."

Bolynne flicked away a tear, and closed her eyes. She blew out all the candles. The shoppers applauded.

"I was— I was," Bolynne said.

"Frantic?" Sugar asked.

"Yes, very much so. I didn't understand why we didn't look in the oven for the cake before the show. Why didn't we Lonny?"

He laughed. "We count on Farina to have the cake baked, that we didn't need to do."

"Yes, that's right." Sugar said, waving Farina on in front of the camera.

She refused. She shook her head no, no. Sugar finally grabbed her arm and pulled her out in front of the camera. "This is Farina Moss. She's my son's girlfriend, and hopefully wife someday, because I want more babies on the farm."

"Four-three-two-one."

"Lemon gelatin, cranberry sauce, and yogurt are the ingredients for this low calorie, light dessert, and so easy to make, and best of all, scrumptious," Sugar said to Chubb, pointing at the camera's red light. It clicked off, and Sugar stepped away from the counter.

"Is the water boiling, Lonny?" Bolynne asked.

"Yes, it is, Bolynne." He turned off the burner.

"I bet if we set the water outside today, it would boil, it's that hot," Bolynne said.

"Did you know that water boils at one hundred fifty-nine degrees Fahrenheit on Mt. Everest? And in London, England, it boils at two hundred twelve degrees?"

"Why the difference?" Bolynne asked.

"The difference is in the elevation. Mt. Everest is twenty-nine thousand feet above sea level, and London is sea level."

"I'll remember that if we ever do a show from Mt. Everest," Bolynne giggled, and said, "I will pour one six ounce box of lemon gelatin into the hot water." She stirred while Lonny measured out the cranberry sauce. "We have a dish of the cooled gelatin." Chubb took a close up of Bolynne reaching for the dish, setting it in front of her.

Lonny said, "I put three fourths cup of whole cranberry sauce into a mixing bowl, and Bolynne will pour in the cooled lemon gelatin," Lonny said.

"Again, we are not adding the cold water to the gelatin, because we want the pie to be plump, not wiggly," Bolynne said, "And speaking of plump, this pie is low-calorie because the last ingredient is one-six ounce carton of plain yogurt." Bolynne smiled.

"We have combined all three ingredients and now will pour it into a large graham cracker crust.   We combined crushed the graham crackers and melted butter and patted it into this pie dish."

"It needs to chill an hour?" Lonny asked.

"Yes, and we have our finished product in the refrigerator."

Sugar brought the pie to them. "Is this whipped topping on top?" she asked. Chubb aimed the camera at the finished product.

"It is whipped topping mixed with cream cheese," Bolynne replied.

"Both lite varieties," Lonny said.

Sugar cut the pie and delivered a piece onto a plate. "Lonny, take the first taste test. I have eaten this before." He took a bite. "Uhmmm. It is good," he praised.

"I'm so glad you like it. I created this out of my own kitchen. Sometimes I want something to eat and when I can't get to the store, I look in the cupboard and just brainstorm and thought, well, I'll try this, got to use up these items before they go bad, and low and behold, sometimes it really comes out good." Sugar ended the sentence with her hands in the air.

"Yes, it did, Sugar," Bolynne said. "What's up on our next show is what we all wait for in summer, is fresh corn. Can't wait."

Chubb followed Lonny and Bolynne passing pieces of the

pie around to the shoppers. Some politely declined a sample; others joyfully accepted. Sugar fed one spoonful to a toddler riding in a cart. He spit it out, but Sugar laughed, wiping his face. Standing and staring at her from the countertop, she looked away from Lee Three. "Oh, that man," she grumbled.

◌

A hand reached over to the power button and the television screen went black. Jo sat back in the chair in the employee lounge, and dialed an extension on the phone to talk to Dix. She imagined his feet were up on his desk, his shirt and tie loose, and he batted at flies with a golf club.

"Caddo," he answered.

"Farina is still in Glassburgh and on a cooking show and has a boyfriend Razzy Martin," she delivered in one breath.

He put his feet down. "That's why she hasn't returned. Maybe she won't."

"Aren't you still curious about that place? Giant chickens and a huge ladybug?"

Dix swung a golf club at a fly. "Of— course."

Jo grinned.

Dix checked his weekend planner on the desk. He frowned. Nothing. He took out of the office to the elevator to ride down to the first floor of the building. Maybe the new receptionist would go with him to Glassburgh. He sure didn't want to spend the weekend with Jo. He punched the elevator button. Jo was okay. She was married, and her husband would have to come along. That man preached investments and saving every nickel and dime earned. Need to live a little, he retorted, while he ate steak and eggs for breakfast and Jo and her husband had a cup of coffee and toast.

Ahh, there she was, the blonde with sparkling blue eyes and bronze tan.

"Have you ever been to Glassburgh? I'm going there this weekend. I'd really like you to come along with me."

"Oh, sorry. I have a wedding to attend."

"Hopefully not yours," Dix whined.

She giggled. "No."

"Well, maybe dinner tonight?"

"Lunch would be better at eleven-thirty. I bring my lunch. You probably go through the lunch line."

Monterey tapped the computer screen. Dix craned his neck to look at it. What he saw was the blueprint of the building with all floors. Orange dots traveled down hallways, in the offices, and outside of the building. Orange dots traveled the sidewalks.

"Wow, this is really a sophisticated piece of technology; I never really looked at it before. A red square appeared. "Wow, what is that?"

"Someone turned on a microwave," she said, scrolling down a list of activities normal to the day-to-day operations of the employees.

"It's that sensitive?"

"It's a smart computer."

"Hey, have it look up Glassburgh. What's so different about it?"

Monterey again touched symbols on the screen. A keyboard appeared, and when she typed, the keys lit up. She read from a screen the size of a CD case, "The founder of Glassburgh contended a skyscraper all glass would be a selling point to bring in businesses, and it worked, but then the culture changed, young people had to leave for better jobs in larger towns. Nevertheless, a new 'hip' culture emerged, selling Glassburgh as the health capital of the United States in the early seventies, and a variety of health food and all-natural stores opened. These went up around the glass skyscraper near downtown, and the glassless side, near the high school and fairgrounds became neglected and became the bad side of town. The hood, sort of."

He folded his arms. "So they thought in the seventies that maybe the lavender haze was healthy. I could see that."

Dix watched Jo step out of the elevator. She marched over to him and announced they were going on an assignment. They needed to be in Glassburgh tomorrow.

"Can Monterey go with us?" he asked.

Jo shook her head, making a weird face. "I suppose if she wants."

"Lunch? Right?" Dix asked Monterey.

"Yes. Eleven-thirty."

He knocked on her desk, and departed with Jo. "What's up?"

She waited until she was out of listening distance of the receptionist. "We're being sent back to Glassburgh to get Farina. Welch wants us to talk with her as soon as possible. If she refuses, we're to get a statement on paper."

"I see. Maybe she is being held there against her will. Good thinking on his part."

"Yes, that is why he is in charge."

Roxy the Hometown Wrestler

In a one-piece red sequined wrestling costume, Roxy Roxalena took down her opponent in the first few minutes of the round. The next opponent came out, she defeated her, and she went through one dozen opponents in one night.

The first year was the easiest. Athletic women from the county participated. It brought such a large crowd the first and second years, the county fair board allowed women from outside the county and state to wrestle her. That brought out some of the toughest women wrestlers in the country. Women drove from all over the United States to challenge her.

Hugh cheered her on, "Hey Sugar, you did it again!"

The Lady in the Ladybug

Applause burst from the bleachers. Hondra, the black widow from Louisiana strutted across the ring, her hair hanging in three braids to her hips, almost touching the black lace around the top of her legs.

Hondra approached Roxy. Cameras flashed almost blinding them as they circled one another. Arms slowly raised and bam, Roxy Roxalena fell to the mat. Hondra bore all her power on top of her opponent, almost pinning her to the mat. The crowd yelled. Roxy popped up and answered. Hondra looked right and left, jabbing both arms out, as if she were attacking two opponents. Maybe it was the camera's flash that confused her. Raising her leg to bring down Roxy Roxalena, Hondra found herself on the mat.

The crowd roared. The referee called it. Roxy Roxalena was the winner again.

Hondra ran out of the ring cursing, "Te batirán algún día! El día viene! Brujas Rojas!"

Roxy bowed for the cheering crowd. Newspaper reporters snapped photos, television cameras followed her, and the press asked her questions.

"Roxy, you are a phenomenon!" Hugh yelled.

She stopped, turned to look at the young man who was yelling to her. "Oh, I have the advantage most of the time, I'm extraordinary."

The newspaper people scribbled down that remark.

"And very attractive," Hugh hollered out to her.

"Oh, thank you." She smiled at Hugh and the cameras flashed.

Hugh followed the press around the ring and pushed his way to Roxy. "Roxy, show me around the fairgrounds?"

She tried to answer him, but he disappeared in the crowd. Television reporters flogged microphones at her face, throwing out question after question. "How tough was Hondra? Would you wrestle her again?"

"I didn't know if I could beat Hondra again. She is tough, but I found her disadvantage."

The Lady in the Ladybug

"What was her disadvantage?" A reporter asked.

"Oh, I can't say!" Cameras flashed in her face. She blinked, trying to focus on the reporter.

"Is she the toughest opponent you have faced so far?"

"Yes, she is. I wish her the best of luck at other matches."

"Who do you think you will wrestle in New York City?"

"I don't know. The Pink Tornado, I'm guessing."

Hugh pushed himself between the reporter and Roxy, facing her. "I'm Hugh Martin… from Texas. Aren't you hungry after all that wrestling?"

"A little bit."

The unsettled crowd herded Roxy, Hugh, the newspaper and television reporters around the ring and bottle nosed them at the door to the dressing room. Roxy squeezed through the men to the locker room door,   and exited the crowd. "I'll wait for you," Hugh said, pulling the door shut, keeping out fans and reporters.

Fifteen minutes later, she appeared in Levis and a high school T-shirt.

"Wow, you look even prettier in that, sweet as sugar," Hugh said.

She blushed, took his arm and they made their way to the midway. The reporters were circled around Hondra, she angrily telling them her account of the match. "Senora loca, que hizo dos, soy yo el unico que vio eso?"

She spotted Roxy and shook her fist at her. Hugh led her away. "You won fair and square, Sugar."

She shook her head in bewilderment. "This is going to be my last year at this match."

"Don't let her discourage you, she's a bad sport."

"I am quitting after this last match in New York City. Now, you are Hugh Martin from Texas. Anything else I should know?"

"I just got out of the Marines, spent a year in Japan."

"It's an awful war. I wish it would end." She noticed the tattoo on his right bicep, an eagle wrapped around the globe.

The Lady in the Ladybug

They stepped over large cables on the ground and entered the midway. Millions of light bulbs hanging from the ceiling of the tents brightened the hundreds of trinkets and stuffed animals. Carneys called out temptations to play their joint. One in a pirates costume declared to Sugar she'd win this game. "Three chances for a sawbuck, hook this little doll for the big doll."

Roxy rolled her eyes. Hugh waved him off. They zipped through the carnival, weaved around the rides of Ferris wheel, whirligigs with people screaming, and a Merry Go Round of beautiful horses. They caught sight of a hotdog stand and sashayed to the back of the line. A Carney carried a box hanging around his neck, and called, "A fin for a dog dragged through the garden!"

Hugh pointed at him with two dollars and the Carney stuffed it into his cotton sash.

The Carney handed to him two dogs topped with onion, relish, tomatoes, peppers, mustard, and a dash of celery salt. Hugh unwrapped one dog and gave it to Sugar. He unwrapped the other and took a bite, smiling as he chewed.

"Good," Roxy mumbled.

"Like 'em dragged through the garden."

"Me too," she winked.

Hugh grinned showing his perfect white teeth with pieces of relish stuck between. "Let's go to the funhouse!"

Roxy licked her fingers and crumpled the wrapper, tossing it into the barrel for trash.

Hugh took her hand and led her up to the line waiting to enter the funhouse and he pulled out a five-dollar bill to pay the entrance fee.

A Carney opened the Z shaped door for them and they plunged inside. Sugar laughed at her big belly and bulging head. Hugh frowned at his big belly and bulging head and grabbed Roxy's hand, and they landed in front of the next mirror. "Mmm, I like this one," he said. They were stick thin and ten feet tall. Roxy pulled him to the next mirror and it rendered them pancake thin, spread over the floor. They shrugged, not very interesting compared to the thousand pieces they found of themselves in the next mirror.

In the one after that, they surrounded themselves and couldn't find the mirror. They stepped further down the hallway hearing giggling and laughing from a couple of young girls.

Hugh searched for Roxy. She reached out to touch him, let him know she was there, but her hand found a black hole. "How is this possible?" she asked.

"Magic mirrors." He stepped up behind her, and tapped on her shoulder. She had only six inches more height than he.

"Where were you?" She plopped her fists on her hips.

"Standing over there behind you."

"Strange."

"C'mon over here," he said.

In the last mirror, they didn't see themselves at all. "Where are we? Where are you?"

"Right beside you, Sugar."

"I see you but not in the mirror."

"Oh, it's the door," Hugh said, pushing it open.

Roxy laughed. Hugh laughed and pulled her over to the rides. "How about a ride on the Ferris Wheel?"

"I haven't been on one since I was small."

Hugh scratched his chin, wondering. "Well, here's your chance."

He passed over money to the Carney. "Have a seat in the gondola."

The ride started with a jerk then it slowly rose higher and higher. "Hey! I see the farm!" Roxy said, looking back.

Taking a quick look he questioned, "Your father is a farmer?"

She smiled. "Papa is a great farmer."

"What's he farm?"

"Everything. Corn, beets, peas, potatoes, turnips, broccoli, carrots."

The Lady in the Ladybug

"Pigs?"

"No, no animals."

"Why?"

"Well…" Roxy began, her eyes rolling around for a logical explanation.

"Cattle and pigs would bring in a lot of money."

The Ferris wheel stopped. They crawled out of the gondola, Hugh pointing, "Freakhouse!"

Roxy looked down. "I don't like that place."

"Why not?"

"I'm a freak."

"Oh," he took her hands into his. "Sugar, I think you are beautiful. You are a nice person, and I'm sure your father is. What's his name?"

"Roz Roxalena. My mama's name is Latty."

"How about looking at the exhibits in the 4-H building?"

She perked up and Hugh offered his arm. They walked over the sod to the building where quilts hung from the ceiling and arts and crafts adorned tables. They walked past the 4-H displays. Many were on buckling up when driving, swimming safety, gun safety, and hunting safety. Barbie and Ken dolls acted in many of the displays. Ken had sported a hunting outfit and held a gun but both hands weren't able to touch the gun. A plastic dog accompanied him.

Barbie sat in her Barbie car with a seatbelt on. Ken didn't fare so well on his side of the display; he was on the ground, dead.

Another Barbie swam in a pool and Ken the lifeguard watched. The rules of swimming in a public pool were posted. Swimming in farm ponds was discouraged. Another Ken was in the pool struggling for air, but still smiled.

Hugh found the display where Barbie was the villain, and he smirked. Barbie only drank soda pop and ate junk food. She had stuffing inside her clothing. She was overweight, but Ken ate fruits and vegetables and was in swimming trunks showing his very slim and trim body.

77

The Lady in the Ladybug

Roxy looked at the time. Papa wanted her home by midnight. Even if she were twenty-three, she had rules of the household.

"Are they getting ready to shut this place down?" Hugh noticed the lights had been flickered.

Roxy nodded. "Think so. They lock it at midnight."

They departed the building walking under a full moon, silently, looking for their cars.

"I need to find a place for the night. Where will you be tomorrow, Sugar?"

"Working on the farm. South of Savoy on Marquez Road, Papa's name's on the mailbox."

"Marquez Road? Where is that?"

Roxy pointed but it was the wrong direction. "Go through the town of Savoy, go five more miles and Marquez Road is on the east."

He winked at her, opened his car, and disappeared inside it. He drove out of the parking lot and Roxy lost sight of him going into the city. She looked down sadly and walked to her parked car. "Could have offered him a room in the house, dummy." She kicked at a can on the ground. She kicked it, again and again. She sighed, looked up at the moon, thinking about another trip to New York City for wrestling these women out for revenge and blood because she won every time. She plopped down into her black four-door car and started the engine.

Papa and Mama didn't come to watch her wrestle. It was odd they didn't. Papa had been getting slower and Mama seemed to be ailing. In past years, they sat on the first row, and cheered the loudest. When she won, she marched over to them and kissed and hugged them.

From the Fairgrounds, she traveled over the river on a wood bridge and turned south on a paved road that went by the junior high school and about one mile later, she drove by Marland High School. That road went straight south through the town of Savoy. Glassburgh grew so quickly that Savoy and Glassburgh had joined. That put Savoy High out of business and those students were bussed into Marland High.

78

The Lady in the Ladybug

High school was a tough time for her, being so much larger than the other students, except Willy, a big Hispanic boy. They palled around all through junior high and senior high. When together, Willy showed Roxy wrestling, like on television, so they could enter in the fair in the summer.

Willy joined the Navy, and saw the world, while she worked on the farm. Once, he mailed her a postcard from Germany. She didn't know where he was now.

She unlocked the house. A light shined in the back bedroom. Papa called out hello. Roxy said hello.

"I might have a visitor tomorrow. His name is Hugh Martin, from Texas. He's very nice."

"Oh," Papa chuckled, happily. "Well, New York City?"

"Yes, I won again."

"You're going with me, right?"

"Depends on how you mother feels."

"Okay, well, goodnight." Roxy went to her room, thinking about Papa using the healing globes of light on Mama several times. They just didn't cure old age.

Rivalry

Sugar thought about Papa. She thought about mama. Seems she thought about Papa more often, and he had said that if something new was going on in town, probably someone was paying for it to happen. Papa was always right, most of the time. Papa was a good man with wisdom handed down from his people. She had scribbled down some of his knowledge of growing corn, potatoes, onions, and much of the other crops.

The Lady in the Ladybug

Their favorite time was during harvest. Little round lights rolled along the rows giving enough light for them to pick the vegetables from one end of the field to the other. That was the coolest time to harvest, and no one was around to watch them. They had no hired help, they were the help, and they changed themselves into 'hundreds.' Papa and mama and she had the ability.

They told no one. They told no one of the oddities on the farm.

Sugar walked across the field in the warm morning sunshine, smelling the earth at the beginning of the day. Nothing else smelled as real or primitive as the earth did on a farm.

The Glassburgh News waited on her cement stoop. A headline spelled out the plan for the new country apartments, and a bigger plan to draw more people to Glassburgh. People who wanted to improve their health and life span by eating healthy organic food sold in the stores grown by major organic producers in the county.

Sugar pondered that statement. Why does someone think Glassburgh needs more people? Who exactly wants more population in Glassburgh? At the end of the article was the name of the company, Green Candy Developers, their web site, and email address.

No one communicated with her to prepare for the promotion. She put down the newspaper, slurped the last two sips of coffee, and headed to the shower. A warm muscle relaxing shower and— her clothing! It was old, too long, too short, too low cut, wrong style of sleeves. She was outdated in the fashion world. Modernize. Go to the clothing stores in town and buy them out. Don't wear old rubber boots with a polka dot dress to see Chris.

"No wonder everyone stared," she mumbled, turning in front of the full-length mirror. She ordered herself, "You could stand to lose fifty pounds."

In the most modern outfit she owned, an old denim miniskirt and bell sleeved red and black polka dot blouse, hoop earrings, and hair pulled into a short side ponytail, she looked in the mirror and bit her lip. A red and black polka dot hat? She snuggled it over her hair.

High heels?

She tried on several pairs, and finally a red pair fit.

"Hhm," she grunted, and out the door she wobbled, stopping in front of the garage.

The '73 convertible hadn't been driven for five years, not since Hugh said he had to go to Texas on business, and never came home. It was his prized possession, he keeping it garaged and covered. Couldn't let dust fall on the red Mustang, no, not at all, and the top had to be up when in the garage, even under a tarp.

Poking buttons on the remote on the key ring, the garage doors slowly raised, and garage lights revealed a thick coating of dust on the plastic. She pulled a rope that raised the plastic up, something Hugh had rigged. She unlocked the car and settled down into the front seat, turning keys in the ignition and hood.

The top went down and she geared into reverse, and crept out of the garage. Now with the breeze in her face, she turned on the radio and tuned to rock.

Sunday afternoons when Razzy was small, she and Hugh would take a ride with the top down and listen to the radio. Razzy held onto his cowboy hat and grinned.

She was grinning at that memory in the sunshine. It was almost noon, a clear sky, a slight breeze—a perfect summer day.

Traffic picked up, people racing to restaurants for lunch. All the marquees bragged up their organic lunch buffet. Offered were all-veggie burgers and all-veggie sandwiches with all-natural cheese and dressing. It seemed the businesses were competing for customers. It wasn't that way last month.

She slowed down at the stoplight in Savoy. A pickup stopped at the intersection to her right. The light turned green, she proceeded into the intersection, and the man in the pickup whistled. He thought she was attractive! She smiled. When was the last time she was whistled at? He looked at her, waving. 'Wow! He really likes me.' She proceeded through the intersection, watching the pickup speed down the street.

At Squarestone Enterprises, the usual handsome door attendant welcomed her. She entered the elevator, grabbing hold of the rail, holding on tight, riding up. It stopped on the second floor and a man in a suit boarded. He talked on his cell phone, only nodding at Sugar when he entered. On up to the second and third, and the door opened and two young women hurried in, out of breath, and punching the lobby button. They demanded it to hurry; hurry down, stammering it would be gone and no one would believe it anyway.

'Fifth floor.' The computerized voice said cheerfully.

Sugar watched the five light up and waited for the door to slide open, hearing the computerized voice warn her to watch her step. Greeted by the receptionist, and queried about her appointment and who with, Sugar pointed at Chris Tatro's office. The receptionist buzzed him. The other receptionists watched her. She looked back at them as they leaned back on their office chairs, watching her with a surprised look, like she were a Christmas Tree on the Fourth of July. Sugar heard one woman whisper that she was the woman on the cooking show. The noise of the cart rolling down the hallway with the usual cookies and lemonade sent some back to attention, and stared at their computer screens.

Sugar knocked on Chris's office door, hearing him tell someone he would call them back later. She smiled, she felt like she were more important than a phone call. He answered the door, he taking a few seconds to recognize her.

"Sugar! Come in," he said, motioning to the overstuffed sofa.

"Thank you, Chris." She sat, relieved to be off her feet, rubbing a foot. No, no thank you." She declined the cookies.

"No? No cookies? Sugar what's with that?"

"Uh—" She rubbed a toe.

"Where's your rubber boots? Floppy hat? Polka dot dress?"

"I need to modernize."

"No, no you don't," he scolded. "Customers recognize you in that. That is your trademark. They expect to see you in rubber boots, not high heels!"

"I'm not in the store now, Chris; I came here to find out what is going on in town. Who is this Green Candy Company and why apartments are being built out in the country on the edge of my farm on Jose´ Quatro's property? Who are they for?"

"I don't know, just a new business in town. Don't worry."

Sugar raised her eyebrows, "Who is promoting Glassburgh for bringing in more people? We have enough people. Yesterday I had to throw a young man out of my store. He bedded down in the watermelon. He wouldn't leave. I had to pick him up and throw him out, physically."

"Really?"

"A wrestling move that I hadn't done in—in twenty-five years. That's not normal for someone to not leave a store."

Chris rubbed his chin, trying not to belly laugh. "Which wrestling move? Airplane spin?"

She whined yes and looked up at the ceiling,

Chris grinned. "Cool."

Sadly, Sugar looked down at the floor. "No, it wasn't cool. It was embarrassing."

Chris typed on his laptop. "I will research this company, Green Candy. See what is going on there. Now, the reason I wanted to see you." He rolled out a large blueprint. "Remodeled store on the glassless side. We need to update with a sandwich bar, snack bar, and coffee bar, we'll win more customers around the school area. Teenagers are eating healthier, statistics show. There aren't any eating establishments for seven blocks from the high school."

Sugar looked at the drawings, then at the cookies.

"Sure you don't want a cookie and ice cold lemonade?"

Sugar squinted. "One." She grabbed the almond flavored with

The Lady in the Ladybug

butter cream frosting and took one bite, but stopped to listen to the honking outside down on the street below. The honking went on and on, like a wedding party passing by, but was stuck in traffic. She fluttered her eyelashes, curious, and walked over to the window. The art deco design on the window obscured her view some, but she thought Bobby was down there. Looked like him. What was he doing? She moved over to a larger diagonal spot of clear glass.

The cookie dropped; Sugar turned around. Her puffy, red embarrassed face felled Chris' smile. He watched her every high heel step out of his office. She clipped the secretaries' desks with clients watching and worried over what had taken place in the office and if it would happen to them. Her heels clunked on the tile floor all the way to the elevator and she frantically punched buttons. When she grabbed hold of the handrail, the secretaries stared at her with staring eyes and puckered lips. Sugar punched the lobby button again and again and talked to it, just like those young women did coming up — they must have seen Chicken Soup! That's why they were in a hurry.

She bailed out of the elevator in the lobby and skidded across the slick marble floor. The doorman quickly opened the door for her and nicely warned her to be careful.

Around the building to Squarestone Park between buildings, she watched Bobby lasso Chicken Soup. Lassoed her like a professional chicken wrangler. He threw the rope up above her head. It spun wide open, and when the forcefulness of the throw peaked, the rope slid over Chicken Soup's head. Bobby tackled the end of the rope to tighten the noose.

People slowed down in their cars, watching, laughing, and snapping pictures from cell phones. Sugar smiled like it wasn't a big deal, but these people had never seen a giant chicken. Sugar commented to the people on the sidewalk.

"Grow Big Sell Big. That's my motto." She pointed like one of those girls showing the prizes on television game shows.

84

The Lady in the Ladybug

They laughed at Bobby holding the rope on Chicken Soup. Laughed at Chicken Soup tugging Bobby across the grass to a bird feeder on a brass pole.

"Razzy is on his way!" Bobby yelled.

Chicken Soup pecked at the seeds in the plastic container and broke it off the pole. Sugar lunged for the broken feeder and tried to reattach it to the pole, only welding could repair it.

"On his way in what?" Sugar asked.

"A— tr—uc—k," Bobby said taking a jarring from Chicken Soup.

Sugar looked relieved, and watched Chris' reaction when he came from around the building to look at Chicken Soup. "She is large." He folded his arms, scrutinizing the situation.

"You didn't believe me?" Sugar asked him.

"Yes, Sugar, I believe everything you say."

She smiled. "Good."

Chris jumped to Bobby's side to hold the rope on Chicken Soup. She pounced on a grasshopper, dragging them across the grass.

Sugar tried to help, only getting in the way, and managed to step out of the way to avoid being knocked down. She pulled her cell phone out of her purse.

"Where are you, son? Really? Bobby and Chris are about exhausted holding onto Chicken Soup. No, I drove … okay, okay... I will." She stuck the phone in her purse. "Razzy is stuck in traffic from an accident on Third Avenue, so he wants me to try to have Chicken Soup follow me home in the car."

Bobby and Chris agreed. That would be a good trick. "That might work. Chicken Soup might think the car is a big bug," Bobby said, almost out of breath.

Sugar fished car keys out of her pocket and headed for the parking lot. Bobby and Chris pulled the stubborn fowl with them and when she saw Sugar in the red car, she took attention. Bobby headed for his pickup and Chris watched them maneuver themselves out of the parking lot, people staring and some speechless.

The Lady in the Ladybug

"Take the alleys," Chris said.

Sugar waved goodbye. They plowed a path through the junk littered alleys behind restaurants; some hadn't been driven through for months. Chicken Soup stopped to sniff the air above the garbage at a Chinese restaurant. "C'mon!" Sugar yelled. Chicken Soup followed on behind a lumber yard. She lowered her head down to the ground and peeked under the fence, listening to the saws rip wood. Sugar hollered at her once more and on she walked until out of Glassburgh, then Savoy.

Following along the dirt roads through the countryside, and through the ditches and creeks, Sugar kept track of her in the rear view mirror and side mirrors. It appeared, even if Chicken Soup were larger in the side view mirror that she was slowing down, getting tired from the long journey. Sugar pulled over, and parked near her field of beets. Chicken Soup bent over and pecked off a dozen beet tops, making it a nice little snack. Her eyes slowly shut, becoming tired.

Sugar's favorite song played. *Keep on Trucking*, the man sang. Out of the seat she crawled and danced. Her hips bounced up and down and around in a circle. She put every inch of her being into the dance, making sure she was using all her muscles. Dance off those pounds she exclaimed. Truckin'.

When the song ended, the DJ did not say who sang the song. For ten years she had liked that song and still didn't know who sang it. Sugar nudged Chicken Soup awake. Slowly opening her eyes, she drifted off once more. Sugar stroked her soft white feathers.

"Sorry Chicken Soup, but we have to get home. C'mon, wake up."

Chicken Soup hanged her head, just not able to wake up.

Don't even think it, but I have to do it. In the car, Sugar geared the shift into in reverse, and backed up closely to Chicken Soup. She put on the emergency brake, and at a few steps from Chicken Soup, Sugar sat on the ground and crawled under her and hoisted her bottom onto the backseat of the car. Having a convertible had an advantage for her today and today only. She swung her large drumsticks around into the backseat.

She pushed Chicken Soup over the folded top, probably bending it, but wanted her to not fall out. She reached for the seatbelts, taking one belt from each side of the seats and clipped them together. Chicken Soup was buckled up and ready to roll.

Sugar kept watch on her chicken sleeping away, not even waking up over the railroad tracks. She peered in the side mirror at Razzy in the pickup, laughing. Farina appeared to be emotionless looking straight ahead at Chicken Soup being bounced around and unaware of riding in a car.

Sugar parked near the thicket and pulled her drumsticks over the side of the car, aiming her large feet to the ground. Nudging her awake, eyes wearily opened and she trotted into her nest in the thicket.

Sugar wobbled into her house, flung off the high heels, rubbed her toes, and went into her bedroom.

Dix shook the map open, searched it, and looked ahead. Jo yawned, checked her hairstyle in the mirror, and peeked at her watch. She eyed Dix, seeing which road he would take, neither remembering which triplet fork in the road they traveled on the last trip to Sands County.

Off the road about twelve feet, a little scene of chairs and tables with flowers in a vase seemed cared for, the grass cut and weeds tamed. A few yards further were a Christmas tree and gifts, and a little red wagon. Jo stretched her neck to gawk at the wagon, trying to decide. Dix pressed down on the brake and looked in the rear view mirror. Jo looked back.

Those scenes were trees grown into the shapes of chairs and tables and flowers in a vase.

"We are not on the road to Glassburgh. We did not see this last trip," Jo said.

Dix squinted at the road, and his eyes followed the cars up on the road; a road that rested high above the trees and curved.

"Ah-hah." **Glassburgh 2 miles** → He turned, stopped, and turned right and climbed the hilly road that curved around Sugar Martin's farm and then away to Glassburgh.

"I don't understand how those trees grow into those shapes," Jo asked.

"You ask a serious question in a place with a purple haze and giant ladybugs?"

She shot her hands up around her head. "You ask that because you can't answer it."

"I will figure it out," he said and slowed when a vintage gas station came into view on the left side of the road, then a roadside park, and past that were a few old two-story houses. The GPS voice said to turn right on Gossamer Boulevard, and sailing through two green lights, Dix saw the big green and purple oval sign high in the sky.

Sugar Martin Organic Food Store 1
Grow Big Sell Big.

He met two teenagers exiting the store with an apple in each hand. Jo walked in behind Dix, he pointing at the huge tomatoes on a black shelf.

"Remember that. They were pretty good."

"Very," Jo said, browsing.

Dix went over to the empty area in the middle of the store. The displays of produce had been pushed to the edges of the building. A pretty girl mopped the area. Dix stepped on the dry path of the floor and approached the girl in a lavender polo knit top. "Do you know where we can find one of your co- workers? Farina Moss? She has been working on the cooking show. You're mopping up after it, I bet? She probably is a messy cook."

The Lady in the Ladybug

"She works at the other store."

"On Turnage Street?"

"Yep." She dipped her mop in the water.

Jo took change from the cashier, and heard the garage doors open. Workers pushed in a giant watermelon. Jo watched, her mouth gaping.

"I gotta see this," Dix said.

The watermelon came in on wheels.

"What's going on?" Jo asked.

"It's a promotion. We cut open the watermelon, and serve it to customers, the first time we did this, the watermelon was emptied in one day."

"This is one freaky place!" Dix bellowed. "Gotta love it though."

"Where is Turnage from here?" Jo asked.

"Six blocks east — turn left on River Street," the girl said, giggling at Dix.

Ordinary buildings, businesses, and houses lined the six blocks. Daycare, a retirement home, a golf course, and a bakery welcomed their customers. A new building went up on a vacant lot, across from a bank. The shadow of the bank immersed a taco shop and a barbershop.

River Street curved right, down a hill, and over Sooner River. Dix turned north again on E.V. Stone Street, a newly laid asphalt street. The glass skyscraper came into view in the northeast. A granite sign listed the businesses in the buildings, occupied with attorneys and accountants, a radio station, a modeling agency, and an oil company.

Dix turned left on Turnage. Sugar Martin's Organic Food Store 2 set on a corner lot with spacious parking. The brick building appeared old and a new plastic banner had been attached over the faded name of its previous life.

Dix walked behind the row of cars along the edge of the parking lot. He checked one tag number. The car that Farina had been assigned to had to be accounted for on this trip. Farina seemed less important, than if she were staying or coming back with them.

The Lady in the Ladybug

They ventured inside the store and encountered the check stand not far from the door. To the left posed the square bins of cantaloupe and longer bins full of watermelon. "These must be the baby watermelons," Dix joked. Jo chuckled. The back wall of refrigerated produce displays sounded thunder and lightning before it sprayed the vegetables. They spotted three short grocery aisles beyond that. Salt, pepper, sugar, and canning supplies all on shelving placed diagonally. To the right of the shelving, the EMPLOYEES ONLY placard on a door shared the wall that cornered the television set. They walked past it, curiously, and lingered awhile. Jo walked to the apple table, admiring the shiny red apples mixed in with green and yellow. A cloth lay on the table. It appeared so unusual that she touched it. Moist, soft, and heavy. She sauntered on over to refrigerated cases adjacent to the office, and discovered huge vegetables and weird looking vegetables, strangely shaped squash and weird colored lettuce. Over to the next display they encountered Farina. She looked up from watching the floor as she walked, her face exploding in surprise.

"Whoa, I didn't expect— to see you— today, or any day," she said.

"Welch sent us," Jo said.

"I know. I neglected Welch's orders, so how much trouble am I in?" She led Dix and Jo to the employees' door. "Just a minute, I need to tell the others where I'll be. Okay?"

"Sure," Dix said. Jo nodded, watching her explain to another worker she had some business to attend to and she could not be bothered.

"I won't be long," she assured the employees.

Farina opened the door for Jo and Dix.

"Welch wants a resignation statement, and the keys to the government car."

Farina sat at the table. "Okay."

Dix and Jo's attention turned to the flowers on the table. She eyed Farina and pointed at the flowers. "What color is this?"

The Lady in the Ladybug

Farina sat, touching the flower vase. "The color is called leck. I was intimidated by a new color myself. It can't be reproduced, it only can be grown."

"Leck," Dix said, frowning. "I took an art class in college, and never can there be a new color. All colors are made of the three primary colors," he scoffed.

Farina popped up off the chair, raising her hands up. "Open your mind to new things, Dix," she scolded, and leaned over and scribbled out her resignation on a form that Jo had slid to her on the table. She pushed the sheet of paper over to Dix. "Okay?"

He smiled. "Keys?"

She laid those on the table with the cell phone.

Jo looked directly into her eyes. "Are you okay, Farina? Everything in order for you? Do you need money, or—"

"No, I am fine. Life is good."

"Nothing keeping you here against your will?" Dix asked.

"Everything is keeping me here. I'd tell you, but you wouldn't believe it. All I can explain to you is that it is very healthy to live in Sands County."

"I'll take that answer," Jo said.

"Good," Farina accepted.

Dix put the resignation in his shirt pocket. He held out his hand for Farina to shake and she accepted. Jo and Farina shook hands and Farina smiled lazily and opened the door, letting Dix out. He pointed out the silly squash, asked how it got in those shapes, and peered back at Jo who slyly put the leck colored flower in her purse. Jo explained how Sugar grew the silly squash. It was simple. She put the growing squash into a clear hose, and arranged it into shapes."

"That's funny," Jo said, following Dix.

"Follow me? Or do you want to take the lead?" he asked.

"You have the GPS," she answered.

The Lady in the Ladybug

Dix in one car, and Jo in the other, they turned out of the parking lot, and onto the street that would lead them out onto the highway, except a minor accident caused a detour.

Dix turned right and on the next block on a corner was another produce store. On the marquee in red, white, and blue and big bold print read **THREE ORGANIC STORES**. Dix parked near the front door.   Jo parked, wondering what Dix wanted at this store.

"Hungry?" she asked.

"No, just want to see what this store has to sell. Coming in with me?"

"I'll stay here."

The set up of the store wasn't as unique as Sugar's store. No funny looking vegetables or thunder and lightning.

He picked up a couple red apples and took them to the cashier, a man about forty, a little chunky, and friendly tapped buttons on the computer keyboard.

"Hello, how are you, today, sir?" he asked.

Dix, reading his name tag answered, "Just fine, Bobby."

"Two dollars please, sir," Bobby requested of Dix.

Dix handed over a five dollar bill, and waited for his change. Bobby also gave him a brochure about the store. It explained how to order online, and promoted the benefits of buying fruit and vegetables from the Glassburgh area. Dix spied the sentence — *The bounty from this county has a special ingredient that can only be found in Sands County, Coronado. Many have been cured of diseases just from eating from Sands County produce.*

"Is that so?" Dix asked.

"Yes, sir, it is. I lived away from Glassburgh, and got very ill. I came back to live here, and I do not have a liver disease now. Thanks to the fruit and vegetables grown here."

"Really." Dix tapped the brochure on the counter.

"Yes, sir, it is true. My doctor can attest to my statement."

"Who owns this store?" Dix asked.

The Lady in the Ladybug

"Lee Three," Bobby said.

"Who is he? Does he sell from his own farm?"

"No, buys from other organic farmers in Sands County, only."

"I was just in Sugar Martin's store; saw nothing about this special ingredient there—"

"No one else put money into an investigation of the asteroid soil. He has credible people who studied it."

"Thanks," Dix said, taking the brochure with him, reading it on the way over to Jo.

He handed the brochure to her. "This guy is trying to capture the market on the health benefits of Sands County. Entice the world to buy his produce."

"And that is bad, how?" She waited for his comeback, but noticed he had spied a limousine parking nearby. Two women emerged from it, wearing sunglasses, and hats, and tight fitting clothing.

"Ah hah!" Dix exclaimed.

Jo looked at him. "Ah hah what?"

"He's got the rich and famous convinced of it."

Jo laughed, shook her head. "Let's go."

⬡

Lee Three scrutinized Sugar's produce, turning an apple over and over.

He won't ever find anything wrong with my produce. I have shining cloths. But, a flash of fear rippled through her about those lying around the workstations. Those shining cloths were used in front of customers daily. She charged toward the workstation where Farina shined apples.

"Farina, Farina …"

She looked up seeing Lee Three in the background snooping in the fruit.

"Hide the shining cloths."

93

Farina put them in the drawer and locked it.

"Are there any others out in sight?" Sugar asked and looked over at the other countertops.

"I'll check it out," Farina said.

Sugar turned around, watching Three looking like a buzzard hovering over prey. His long beaky nose and bony arms and legs, and his black suit coat two sizes too large just hanging off him.

"What's he looking for, Sugar?" Farina asked.

"Imperfections. He won't find any."

He plopped his fists on his bony hips and walked around. He turned and bumped into Atla.

"Excuse me," he said.

"Certainly." Atla handed a paper to Sugar. "Here it is."

"Thank you." Sugar read the report and puckered her lips, showing excitement in her eyes.

"Sales have been excellent!" She felt a tap on her shoulder, and turned to a woman wearing a cowboy hat and boots, Levi's and a western shirt. "Is the rodeo in town?" Sugar asked, chuckling.

"It sure is," Appalonia said, laughing. "Silas is out checking the camper tires in the parking lot."

Sugar hugged Appalonia Green. "It's so good to see you, App."

The hug ended with a serious statement from Appalonia, "We're here for a reason," she said sadly. "Silas has liver problems. We read an article in the Ft. Worth newspaper about Glassburgh and how the fruit and vegetables will cure you of anything wrong."

"Newspaper?" Sugar asked.

"We've been reading it in several newspapers in Texas and Oklahoma."

"Really." That Green Candy company came to mind; Chris never related to her who they were or what they were. "Do they mention my stores?"

"Uh," she searched her memory. "No. I read carefully and didn't see it."

The Lady in the Ladybug

"Well, that's good, seems a little farfetched to me. Oh, but what about Silas? What sort of liver problem is it? Is he on medication?"

Appalonia answered, looking bewildered. "The doctor has him on pain medication, and pills to keep him from becoming nauseous."

"I'm sorry," Sugar said. "Let's go into the office."

"We're coping, Roxy. I just keep remembering us picking corn every summer, and all those apricots!"

They giggled on the way to the office. Sugar let App go in first, and let her sit. Sugar sat in her office chair, laughing again at the dear memory. A man peeked into the office from the side of the door.

"Silas!" Sugar shouted. She popped up and hugged him noticing his jaundice. Sugar towered over the man and surrounded him with her hug.

"We want to take you out for lunch, Roxy," Silas said.

"Oh, that would be a welcome treat."

Sugar picked up her purse, and with Silas and Appalonia leading the way to the front door, they walked past women in the most recent fad of clothing, sunglasses, and reusable shopping bags.

Out in the parking lot were cars with out of state license plates. Texas and Colorado, Sugar noted, which wasn't unusual, but Florida, California, New Jersey, and Tennessee plates with back seats packed with boxes and clothing racks full. Campers and vans from other states pulled in and parked. Silas opened the pickup door for them.

"You are doing great business, Roxy," Silas said.

"Looks that way today."

The pickup without camper traveled across the parking lot and onto the boulevard. Sugar looked at cars in the parking lots at businesses on both sides of the street. All were busy. The windows on the businesses were sparkling clean. Posters in all the windows claimed the best deals in town. The pawnshop even looked cleaner and several out of state cars were parked around it.

Silas turned to their favorite family restaurant sandwiched between a bakery and small boutique with the lawn mowed recently.

"Do you remember anything else about these newspaper articles?" Sugar asked.

"Well," Silas chuckled, "One fella moved to Sands County after being away, and he told the reporter that he felt better and his blood work was better. This got my attention and this guy's name is one that sticks with you, Bobby Click."

"What?"

"Yes, Bobby Click."

Sugar held her forehead. Silas opened the pickup door, waiting for her, waiting for her to step out.

"What's wrong?" Appalonia asked.

Sugar stepped down out of the pickup. Her face reddened, seeming angry and frustrated. "Bobby Click works for me on the farm. He has a part-time job in a store of my competitor. Oh, why did I hire him? What was I thinking?"

"Maybe he is a good person, Sugar."

Sugar flipped open her phone and then shut it. "I don't know what to do."

The Lady in the Ladybug

Strange Trees

"Deep in the woods, the man of the house of Roxalena unlocked the front door one spring morning after the last snow paralyzed the occupants in the high hills on the western horizon—that would be San Amez," Dix read.

Jo eyed him and his feet; she watched where they would go next. Not on her desk, she glared. He repositioned himself in the chair, sat up from slouching, and his feet danced on the carpet. He wanted so badly to plop up his feet on the desk. Jo wondered why he wasn't at his desk typing out reports. That annoyed her more than his singsong reading voice.

"Moy Roxalena thrust open the wood door stuck from months of wet snow piled against it. He squinted in the bright sun, and stepped over the melting snowdrifts, heading down to the river for water.

Sticking out of the snow was a little doll. It dropped from his daughter's hands when he called her to the house when a high wind hit and the temperature fell before the first great snowstorm of winter in November. He pulled the doll out of the slushy snow, and noticed the trees. That tree, he grinned, it had grown into the shape of the doll."

He continued reading the research paper he found at the San Amez Library about the tree festival. Jo typed on her computer keyboard and ignored him.

"Summer came and went, and autumn brought orange and red leaves covering the ground. Moy Roxalena put on the ground an old shoe, and a leaky teakettle. Anxiously awaiting spring, hoping the trees would again grow into the shapes put before them.

The warm spring arrived late in May, and he showed his family the trees grown into the shapes of the old shoe and teakettle. Every autumn afterward, the Roxalena children put something before the trees. They never understood how the trees grew into shapes, but every spring, when they could emerge from the house that shielded them from harsh winter storms, they delighted to see the trees grown into marvelous shapes.

Little Sod Roxalena told his friends every year about the trees.

Sod's son, Roz, farmed near those trees. In autumn, he let anyone set down an object in front of the trees."

'What kind of trees are these?' People asked.

Roz didn't know. They had been on this hillside since his grandfather lived in the old house built into the hill.

'What makes them grow into shapes? How do they do it?' People asked.

Again, Roz said he didn't have the answers. It was a mystery, a fun mystery.

Little Roxy put down her dolls and toys in autumn, and wrote on pieces of paper the days to wait in the house until spring. She made her own little calendar. Papa told her that day was the last snow of the season. She circled the day, the day she could go outside to see the trees.

It arrived along with three bulldozers mauling down trees, hillsides, forests on all sides of the Roxalena farm. A man in a suit showed papers. The city edged its way closer to the farm of Roz Roxalena—that would be Glassburgh," he said to Jo.

She ignored him and answered her phone.

"Listening to the dozer and trucks, watching houses and buildings popping up onto the land beside their farm, Roz loaded up his wife and little Roxy. They moved into a new house right in the middle of Sands County, just a few miles from that acreage.

Her trees! Roxy cried she had no trees. Roz patted her head.

Globes of Light

Carrying a silver pail with a lid snapped tight, Sugar walked across the patchy grass in the RV Park and knocked on Silas and Appalonia's camper door. She heard the doors unlatch and open, and stepped down when the outer door swung open.

"Roxy, come in," Appalonia said.

She slowly climbed the steps and held onto the railing, and looked for Silas. Cookie, their female Yorky, ran to Sugar's feet and sniffed.

"Where's Silas?"

"Sleeping."

"Oh, I brought this for him."

"I'll give it to him when he wakes," Appalonia said.

"Uh, can't—"

"Give what to me?" Silas sleepily asked.

"Stay there, Silas." She took her pail and pushed through the narrow hallway and up the two steps to the bed. "Lie down again."

"What for, Roxy?"

"Just lay down, please."

Watching Sugar snap off the lid on the silver pail, light burst from it, and Sugar reached in and showed a handful of globes of light to him. She placed them on Silas's chest.

"What are these?"

"Globes of light. They're here on earth to heal. They fell from the asteroid that exploded over the county, way back."

"Say that again," Silas said, wiping perspiration off his brow.

"These heal, not the food in Sands County, but these globes. You have to swear not to tell anyone."

"Roxy, I know you want Silas to be well, but this is—is crazy."

"Not a word, okay?" She gathered the globes as if they were eggs in a hen house, and deposited them in the pail and snapped on the lid. "I'll check on you later."

"You're always welcome," Appalonia said.

"Please believe me. Papa wouldn't lie about something like this."

"No, he wouldn't, Roxy. Whenever we came for a summer visit, things around here were a little different, but you and your father made it all seem…necessary." Appalonia opened the door.

Sugar petted Cookie one last time before leaving.

"That was strange," Silas said. "I know some of the strange things you told me about the farm, but this takes the cake."

The Destruction

Chicken Soup and her chicks walked a row of corn, pecked the ground, and scavenged fat little bugs and worms. She eyed a grasshopper and snatched it off the stalk, scattering leaves and more grasshoppers to the ground.

The chickens weaved in and out of the rows of corn inspecting each stalk for another delicacy of green. Mazing their way to the end of the cornfield, Chicken Soup poked her head through the last few rows. Feathers ruffled up and not quite laid back down when she stood beak to pincer with Cleopatra. That pest opened and closed her pincers, preparing a snap. Chicken Soup had experienced it once, only once. It wouldn't happen again, and she stepped up to her, hissing, scratching the dirt, and let out a high pitched squawk.

The showdown ended with a strike of thunder. A multitude of grasshoppers struck the ground. Stalks fell; stems cracked, and toppled like dominoes under the weight of the massive invasion.

Cleopatra and her young buzzed in the air above the destruction. Chicken Soup and chicks retreated to their nest which was not immune to the 'hoppers' invasion. They ran toward a noise in the field, and wings flapped away the cloud of grasshoppers.

100

The Lady in the Ladybug

Cleopatra flew around the picker making a noise of flunk, clunk, clunk—its pointy cones at the sides augured the crop through the machine and into a wagon on the backside. Razzy kept his eyes on the side mirrors of the corn picker, a cross between a tractor and a stealth bomber, slowly making a path through the stalks.

Chicken Soup and the chicks ran in front, and Razzy almost ran over the last chick. He stomped the brake, and climbed down off the picker. "Whoa! Where did those all come from?"

He climbed back up on the machine and helplessly watched. Striking the front of his cell phone, he called Farina. "Look outside! Look at the grasshoppers!"

"Where did they all come from?" She stared out the back porch window while they devoured the leaves and petals off the climbing roses. They ate bark. They stripped leaves off the trees. "Razzy, come home! This is awful!"

"Call mother!" Razzy told her.

Farina scrolled down to Sugar's number and waited while the phone rang three times. Sugar answered happily.

Farina bleated out, "Grasshoppers. Thousands of them—eating everything!"

"Say that again?"

"Sugar, come home, Razzy and I don't know what to do." Sugar scrambled out of the office. She heard her name called and thought—not now. Her heels clomped on the cement driveway, and she tried to avoid the cracks and seams. Air whooshed over her sounding like the words, Ssssssugar- Ssssssugar.

Appalonia and Silas popped out of their pickup. They waved her down.

"Where are you going in such a hurry?"

"An e—mer—gency!"

"Like what?" Silas asked.

She slowed down and caught her breath, "come—with me— you'll see— I'm thinking— sab— sab—otage."

The Lady in the Ladybug

Appalonia looked at Silas for his reaction. Neither knew what to say to her. They only followed her to the car, and piled in the back seat of her low-slung car. Sugar plopped in the driver's seat and squealed tires out of the parking lot. Heads turned. She heard exclamations of 'slow down,' and 'you'll get there.'

"It must be bad," said Silas, "I've never seen you in such a hurry."

"It is bad—thousands of grasshoppers are consuming the farm."

"That is reason to be frantic," Appalonia said.

Sugar looked in the rear view mirror at her. She took a shortcut around the city via an alley behind a furniture store and onto a country road. "I think the grasshoppers were released."

"How will you prove it?" Appalonia asked.

Sugar pouted angrily. "I—I don't know."

"You need to hire an expert," Silas said.

Sugar arrived in Savoy and turned to go to the four-way stop. Posted on a metal sign in large, red letters declared San Amez as seventy-five miles. Sugar looked over at Appalonia. "Jo and Dix, that's who I'll call. Here," she handed her cell phone to her. "Find the number for the USDA."

Appalonia scrolled through it, clicked on it, and handed the phone to Sugar. She pulled off to the side of the road. "Yes, I need to talk to Jo and Dix in the USDA."

A young woman asked who was calling.

"Sugar Martin. They know who I am, Monterey."

She replied they were answering— "Now."

"Agent Harris, speaking, how may I help you?"

"Jo? It's Sugar, Sugar Martin. Know anything about outbreaks of grasshoppers on organic farms? Or know of how someone can buy thousands of grasshoppers and release them?"

Strange Trees,
continued

Dix continued reading, "Roz opened one hand to reveal—"

"Grasshoppers," Jo said.

"No, Jo, seeds. Roxy squealed that her father had saved some seeds." Dix watched Jo to see if she paid attention and she didn't, she only typed in grasshopper invasion, grasshopper farms, and the computer voice suggested other searches.

"Grasshoppers? Where?" He asked, and scooted the chair closer to the monitor.

"What happened?"

"In a minute we'll have pictures," she said. Jo clicked on their email inbox and waited for Sugar's cell phone pictures to arrive.

Dix stared in shock. "Whoa, that's bad."

Green grasshoppers covered the hood of her red car in one photo. In the next, a silvery cloud rolling on the highway and billowing over the fields.

"Unbelievable." She turned to face Dix.

"Show this to Welch, it kind of does fall under our jurisdiction."

She forwarded the email, and trotted to Mr. Welch's office. Dix followed, knowing where she was headed. She knocked and went in.

"I see it," Welch said.

"Ms. Martin fears it is sabotage."

He shook his head in debate. "Organic farms are subject to insect invasion."

"Yes, sir, we realize that, and know that Sugar has every device known for organic farming to prevent this tragedy. Her family has been farming for centuries—with great success, and she—"

"Jo," he held up his hand to interrupt, and handed to her a key to a government vehicle. "Both of you go back to Glassburgh, again. First, see about this grasshopper problem, and this fairy tale that eating food from Sands County can cure diseases."

"Yes, sir." Jo happily trotted out of Welch's office with Dix.

The Shining Cloth

Yawning, Atla unlocked the store at eight a.m. She ambled into the office and flipped on the lights in a sigh, turned on the copy machine in a grunt, and powered the computer. The fax machine spewed out paper. She called the store on Gossamer Street and asked the manager for her sales of the previous day.

Sugar walked in, sat down two cups of Irish Cream flavored coffee and two sugar donuts. Slurping the coffee, she walked out of the office to the backroom. Apricots the size of a baseball awaited the touch of a shining cloth.

Sugar whistled all the way into the break room, opened the supply closet, and searched every nook and cranny for them.

"Okay, where are they?" She searched shelves, drawers, and scrutinized every employee locker. Sighing deeply, her breath shortened into panic.

Trotting out of the break room, she toured the television set and didn't see them hanging over anything or tossed in behind something. She had to investigate every possibility, but she gave up and enlisted Atla's help. She plopped around the corner of the office and tromped up the office steps.

"Shin-ing clo-ths! I-I can't f-find them."

Atla looked up to see a distressed out of breath Sugar. "I'll help you look. Then if we don't find them, I'll start calling."

Atla scoured the check stands. Sugar pursued the shining cloths on or under the fruit bins, the potato bins, and the vegetable displays.

The Lady in the Ladybug

Both took off in separate directions and ended up in the backroom. Sugar searched around the garage door. Atla went into the cooler and moved boxes on shelves. Sugar hunted below and under the pipes, floor scrubber, sink, and shelving round the corner. Atla and Sugar came face to face from the areas they examined.

"I don't think they are here," announced Atla. "I'll start calling the employees."

Sugar stood with hands on her hips, lips clenched, and eyes tearing. She returned to the break room and opened up the lockers. They had to be here, she mumbled. A couple of lockers had padlocks.

She rummaged in drawers that she hadn't opened since the day she walked into the store. She hadn't taken the time to clean out the drawers. In them was an interesting mix of coffee creamer packets, bandages, tape measures, screwdrivers, spoons, pennies, pencils, and notepads with the former store's logo and phone number. Everything but the shining cloths.

The year she invented them, Razzy was in fourth grade. Everyone said the Osage orange hedge apples kept away spiders, and keeping away insects was a full time job. Out in the orchard, she and Razzy picked them and loaded a truck full. Sugar chopped them up and stuck them into smaller crevices in the foundation and garage. She discovered through trial and error of how to get that unique oil out of a hedge apple. She ground the rind to create the shining cloth fabric, wove them on a small loom, and injected the oil into one finished cloth.

That summer she discovered that the hedge apple had many secrets.

Razzy played around the tree, entertaining himself while she picked. She scolded him for running into the road on the edge of the orchard. Grabbing him out of the road many times, he became angry and threw a hedge apple at a car going by. The hedge ball missed, but Sugar's hand did not miss Razzy's butt.

He cried, then what he saw, he wiped his eyes and pointed. The hedge apple struck the trees across the road. Those sensitive trees folding their leaves together revealed an open arch in the rock wall.

Small round globes of light rolled on the grass. Light swirled among tiny flecks of silver inside the globes, almost like a snow globe. Razzy gently held one in his hand. Sugar picked one up, examining it closely.

"What are they?" Razzy asked.

"Globes of light."

Sugar nodded at Razzy and they let the globes in their hands go with the group slowly rolling away. Papa knew what they were and where they came from. Papa knew everything about the farmland and Sands County. Papa knew the story about the asteroid that exploded one night many years back, handing the story down from great-great grandfathers.

Atla flew into the back room. "I've called everyone. No one claims to know anything."

Farina and a couple more employees walked in the break room. Tess stared at her open locker.

"I'm frantic, girls, the shining cloths are missing. I've been tearing this room apart looking for them." Lips pouting, Sugar marched out of the break room to the backroom and heard Razzy's pickup at the back door. Sugar pulled the rope to open the garage door and stood on the dock. He turned off the engine, jumped out of the cab, and glanced up at her.

"Want to talk about it?"

"Sabotage again!"

Razzy frowned, staring into his mother's watery eyes. He lifted a box out of the pickup bed. Divided equally among the boxes were summer squash, acorn squash, spaghetti squash, and butternut.

Sugar lifted the boxes onto a cart and wheeled it out into the store, meeting Lonny and Bolynne at the television set.

Lonny ran over to Sugar and insisted he push the cart. Sugar giggled and let him. She saw another poster that Chris put up yesterday. Sugar stood in the background holding a freshly baked pie, a row of green crops behind her. In front of her were Lonny and Bolynne in the kitchen each holding cooking utensils.

Sugar Martin's Cooking Show in black letters at the top, and smaller letters spelling out Lonny and Bolynne crossword puzzle style.

L

O

B O L Y N N E

N

Y

Sugar plopped her hands on her hips and tilted her head to one side. How odd it was that their names were almost matching letters. How odd that they paired up to work in the store. How odd was it that they were in the store when Chris talked about the cooking show.

Getting ready for another show, Sugar watched Bolynne pluck food out of the refrigerator. Lonny elected their favorite cooking pans and utensils. Next, he measured out ingredients; Bolynne mixed. She poured the batter for a cinnamon pumpkin cheesecake into a dish. Lonny shaved chocolate into a small bowl, eating more than he shaved. Bolynne scooped up a spoonful and carefully ate it, not letting any little morsel fall onto her clothing.

Chris and Chubb appeared at the set. He handed out the scripts for the show, one for Sugar and one each for Lonny and Bolynne.

"Like the new poster?" Chris asked Sugar.

"Yes, very much. I look so much thinner."

"I am putting a larger poster in the store 1. I thought we might do a mini show over there sometime and have an audience of only high school students."

"Really?" Asked Bolynne, her face aglow.

"Yep. You two are quite a sensation with the younger crowd, if you didn't know."

Lonny pointed at the poster, "I'm sure they watch it for the ladies, not me."

"You two work well together, like-like gears in a clock," Chris said.

Sugar rolled her eyes at that comparison.

Bolynne fluffed her hair.

Atla appeared at the set, cornering Chris and Sugar. She read a list of new items to be set up in store 1. Sugar looked at the list, mumbling "A new organic coffee bar, a snack bar, and luncheonette."

"With several hundred new high school students enrolled, the students need a place to hang after school," Atla reminded.

"This is something we think will be a success," Chris pointed out.

"These students don't need an ice cream parlor after school, but good nutritious snacks,"

Atla said and continued, "With all these new items in the store, and a facelift or two, it will be the hip place to go." Paged to the phone, she cheerily marched to the backroom.

"That's true," offered Lonny. "Getting ice cream and burgers after school every day will put on a lot of belly flab."

Bolynne instantly looked down at her stomach.

Shopping carts whizzed past. Chubb announced, "Fifteen minutes until Sugar Martin's Cooking Show."

Inspecting last minute details, Lonny, Bolynne, and Sugar spot-checked all the ingredients.

Lonny pointed at small bowls and then marked them off the list. Bolynne signed off on the required utensils for the recipe, and Sugar reread her introductory paragraph.

They looked up when they heard a group of people around the corner, sounding as if they had a party going on, they tooted horns, carried balloons and bouquets of roses. The eldest woman requested of Sugar to find Atla Flowers.

The Lady in the Ladybug

"What's going on?" Sugar asked.

"We are the awards committee for the tree festival, and—"

Sugar listened to her explaining and picked up the intercom phone and paged Atla to the set.

Atla came around the corner, seeing the group, and slowed her pace to figure out what she was encountering.

"I'm Atla Flowers, how may I assist you?"

"Atla, I am Mrs. Chaledonci and we are the awards committee for the tree festival, as I was saying—" she handed her a balloon and a bouquet, "You have won first place."

Atla popped her mouth wide open. "My entry won?"

"Congratulations!" The committee echoed.

Atla grinned.

"Wow!" Sugar said. "What object is your tree?"

Atla's smile fell. Parts of several dolls were put together covered with a polka dot dress, rubber boots, and a straw bonnet. The doll's pose of hanging onto the underneath of a huge ladybug brought a few laughs from Atla and her friends gluing the doll together.

"You."

"Me?"

"Yes. You."

Lonny and Bolynne surrounded Sugar and Atla, shaking their hands. "We'll be at the ceremony filming and interviewing," Lonny said.

"How wonderful," Mrs. Chaledonci said. "Lee Three will be the master of ceremonies and award you the first place trophy."

"Lee Three!" Sugar growled.

"Yes, one of our much respected businessmen. Is that a problem?"

"He is our competitor," Sugar snarled, and stomped away.

Mrs. Chaledonci objected to her comments and stood up straighter to sound her judgment. "Well, you will just have to be adult about it, won't you!"

"Yes, I'll be very adult."

The Lady in the Ladybug

The Tree Festival

Eleven trees back from the platform, people collected around Sugar Martin hanging from a huge ladybug. The tree brought a laugh, and then wonderment. The tree had recreated the dots on the polka dot dress and the straw hat amazingly was small leafless branches. Boots grew smooth. The leaves had tightly overlapped that gave the look of rubber.

The trunk of the tree wasn't visible in the live artwork, and the belly of the ladybug with legs folded against the body was fascinating.

Mrs. Chaledonci stepped up onto the platform. She tapped the microphone. "One hundred years ago, an asteroid hit this county, leaving some extraordinary objects. Tree saplings with the characteristic ability to grow into an object set before it, have fascinated us, and we took that fascination and turned it into art. People were afraid at first, but our ancestors were not ones to destroy what was different. Wherever you see a tree grown into the shape of a house or old antique car, you know it is an 'asteroid tree.' Welcome to the nineteenth annual tree festival! Waiting are you? Waiting to hear your name called to the platform as this year's winner? Only the first place winner knows. Second place through tenth is still a secret."

The awards committee carried plaques, flowers, and balloons to the platform.

"Our master of ceremonies, Mr. Lee Three," she announced.

"Welcome to the nineteenth annual tree festival—Atla Flowers is—" Three pulled a pair of reading glasses out from his tuxedo's breast pocket, unfolded them, and squinted at the paper. He slid the glasses on, and blinked his eyes. "What? That can't be!" He swatted the program on the podium and flipped off the paper with his middle finger.

"Mr. Three? Is there a problem?" Mrs. Chaledonci asked, frowning.

Three's face turned pleasant, "Certainly not. Just killed a pesky flying thing."

"Please continue."

Three stuck his nose in front of the paper. "First place winner! Everyone ready? Eleven trees that way is Sugar Martin hanging onto the ladybug in-flight. Atla Flowers from Glassburgh is the first place winner!"

The crowd applauded, though they looked for Atla to walk up onto the platform, no one appeared to accept the award. Three looked over the crowd; he waited a few seconds. "Okay, not here," and he read the second place winner. "Tim—"

"Atla? Atla please come up on stage," insisted Mrs. Chaledonci. She pushed the flower bouquet at Three to give to her. He wiggled his nose to stifle an itch from the scent of the perfumed roses. He crinkled his nose to the left and to the right.

"Ahhhchew!" The sneeze sounded painful, and he dropped the bouquet. One hand flew up to his nose, the other pulled out a handkerchief from his tuxedo pocket. He blew his nose loudly broadcasting the honking goose call all over the tree festival.

People snickered. Some laughed. Farina and Razzy glanced at each other, giggling, until she looked closer at the handkerchief. She squinted at it, took a few steps up to the platform, and looked back at Razzy, she motioning him to step closer. Jo curiously frowned and followed Razzy.

"That's a shining cloth he just blew his nose on!" Farina told him.

Bobby pushed his way through the crowd. He looked up at Three snorting and sneezing.

Farina cupped her hand over Jo's ear and whispered.

Applause began in the rear of the tree park. Everyone ahead of the sea of applause turned to look.

Sugar and Atla had arrived and were weaving through the crowd clearing a path for them. When close enough for Three to see them, he turned stone cold and picked up the fallen bouquet of roses and waited for Atla to arrive on the platform.

He handed to her the flowers and read, "Congratulations, Atla, on winning first—first—ahh-chew! place."

Up came the shining cloth and to his nose he stuck it, blowing and wiping. Sugar stared at her shining cloth covered with mucus.

"My shining cloth. He stole my shining cloth!" she pointed at him.

Atla noticed Sugar pointing. She spoke into the microphone. "It is a complete surprise for me and for Sugar."

Mrs. Chaledonci cocked her head. She stared at Atla.

Sugar stepped up to the platform. "I spent many years, many experiments making those out of the least expected thing, a hedge apple. Don't blow your snotty nose on it." Sugar took one step up.

"Ladies and gentlemen, the woman who inspired my tree, the lady in the ladybug, Sugar Martin," Atla said. The crowd applauded. She took her bouquet and plaque, and hurried off the platform. Sugar had arrived on the third step when she grabbed her chest and bent over. The crowd waited and watched. Sugar straightened up and took one more step, but toppled over. People gasped.

Atla dropped the flowers and plaque, and tried to grab Sugar's arm, but she proved too heavy, and she let go. Sugar rolled off the steps and fell a few feet to the ground.

"We need an ambulance! It's Sugar Martin, she's collapsed," announced Mrs. Chaledonci.

With tears streaming down her face, Atla watched Dix and Mal controlling the crowd. Jo pushed through, and trotted over to Razzy. "Don't move her," she ordered. "Don't try to get her up, wait for the EMTs!"

Razzy wiped his eyes.

The Lady in the Ladybug

Dix tapped Jo on the shoulder. "We need to send this crowd home." Mal followed the lead and showed his ID badge. He put his hands out to show his authority to kindly depart the park. The festival goers turned away and slowly walked out. Jo stepped outside the fence to encourage more people to leave the ceremony.

An ambulance siren wailed. It began out on the highway, and came closer. Doors opened and closed and the clanking of a gurney rolled over the ground.

Two EMTs stopped, asking for the patient.

"She's here," Dix pointed.

The EMTs grabbed a neck brace off the gurney, and wrapped and secured it around Sugar's neck.

One EMT checked her mouth and throat for foreign objects. The other slid a slick plastic backboard under Sugar.

The male EMT wrapped a cuff around her arm, and turned on a small machine. It read blood pressure. It was 145 over 70. "Normal," he remarked and the readings of respiration and pulse were reported to the hospital.

The EMTs counted to three, and slid her onto the gurney, pulling straps over Sugar and secured them. Magically, the gurney rose with the buzzing sound of the battery operated hydraulic. They pushed her out of the park and to the ambulance.

Razzy followed and everyone slowly walked behind him. They pushed the gurney inside the ambulance, and the female EMT sat beside Sugar, and the male EMT closed the doors. Razzy glanced at the man who had been standing behind the open ambulance doors. The siren bleated. Razzy looked back and stared at the man.

"Dad?"

"Hello, Razzy."

Hugh watched Razzy and Farina run to their vehicles, and follow the ambulance.

Hugh Comes Home

Sugar's chart, only a few papers thick, lay on the counter. The nurse attached pads to her chest, blood pressure cuff wrapped, and airway checked. With oxygen saturation checked, they all read good. The heart rhythm was normal.

Razzy walked into the room.

"And you are a relative?" the nurse asked.

"Son."

"Okay, you may sit over there." She pointed at a folding chair.

"Can my girlfriend come in?"

"Yes, I limit it to two."

Razzy looked out into the hallway, "Farina!" He curled his index finger at her. She walked inside and closed the door.

"Her vitals are good," the nurse said. "Don't understand why she's not responding. Looks like she landed on her left side. Bruising is appearing and there's a small cut on her elbow." The nurse picked up the phone and paged the doctor. "Doctor Marquit, please come to ER."

"She just went down at the tree festival," Razzy said. "Don't know why. Well, it's a long story, she might have been upset over something she saw."

The doctor walked into the emergency room, nodded hello to the nurse, shook hands with Razzy.

The nurse explained her findings while he listened to Sugar's heart, lungs, and pushed on her abdomen.

Gently sliding her eyelids up, he shined a small light into her pupils. He felt her ankles. "I want a CT scan, and complete blood work." He looked at her file and grimaced. "She hasn't had any blood work since 1983? Hmm."

Razzy checked his cell phone. "Mother never went to the doctor much,"

"I see that. What happened to her?"

The nurse explained while a lab tech entered with a plastic tote. He filled two tubes of blood. Two X-Ray techs walked in, unlocked the wheels on the gurney, and pushed Sugar out into the hallway. Through two double doors that opened with a touch of a button, they wheeled Sugar into the X-Ray room.

Bobby, Jo, Atla, Dix, Mal, Lonny and Bolynne sat in chairs in the waiting room. Mrs. Chaledonci appeared, a little disgusted looking. She tapped her fingers together while she sat. "What happened? How did it all happen? I don't understand. Why did the tree festival get ruined? I told Ms. Martin to behave in an adult manner. I presume she doesn't get along with Mr. Three?"

Mrs. Chaledonci didn't receive a response, except from Dix. "I doubt she planned on passing out."

Razzy sauntered into the waiting area. Everyone gave him their undivided attention, waiting for the news.

"She still is unconscious. But, she is doing okay.'

"Unconscious?" Atla asked.

"Don't know why. They are doing tests. CT, blood work."

A couple came down the hallway. They stopped sharply when they found the waiting area full. Appalonia spotted Razzy.

"How is your mother?" Silas asked him.

"Unconscious. That's all I know."

Silas nodded at Razzy, and coaxed him around the corner. "Razzy, find the globes of light and heal your mother with them. She used them on me. It worked."

A man passed Silas and Razzy. "How have you been, son?" Hugh asked.

Silas stepped away.

"I came back to talk to your mother."

"Oh? She's not your wife, she's my mother."

"I bought a house in Houston for her. She needs to quit this farming business and settle down."

Razzy frowned. "Really. How about you? Are you going to settle down?"

"I bought a nice house for your mother. She can have a house cleaner if she wants. I'm only thinking about her health and her future."

Razzy's eyes danced, searching for the right attitude, and words. "Gee, dad, maybe she doesn't want to live in a big house in Houston with a house cleaner. Maybe she likes living on the farm. And what's in it for you?"

He opened his mouth not able to give an answer to Razzy's question. "I'll be back later to talk to Sugar."

Razzy took long steps over to the chairs and sat. Red faced, digging his hands into the arms of the chair, holding himself in place while his father departed the hospital. His frustration that began the day his father disappeared, surfaced. The family business needed tending to, and Sugar learned quickly, was strong and smart. He popped off the chair, headed down the hallway, and found Farina at the vending machines.

"Want a pop?" Farina asked.

"No," Razzy said, lips clenching. "Let's hurry back to the ER."

She put her coins in a pocket and walked with him, and met the nurse in the hallway.

"Razzy, we are admitting her for observation. It is possible we will transfer her to San Amez later."

"What for? Tests?"

"If she doesn't gain consciousness in an hour."

"She will," Razzy said.

The Lady in the Ladybug

Healing

Walking into the dark house, Razzy and Farina flipped lights on, unbelieving Sugar was absent from the home. On the couch Razzy sat, hands propping up his chin, elbows poking into his knees. He stared into nothingness. Farina sat beside him, slipping her arms around his waist. She laid her head on his shoulder.

"Do you know about the lights? The globes of light?" he asked.

She straightened up, thinking. "No."

"Grandpa Roxalena had complete control over them." Razzy cupped his hands. He tightened them into fists. "Papa said…"

Farina raised her eyebrow, warily eyeing him, wondering about his demeanor. He stood, walked around the couch and outside. She popped up, keeping him in sight while he walked outside across the front yard and into the plowed under cornfield. A large golden harvest moon raised above the horizon painting hushed light on the ground. She stepped outside. The color of the ground remained a secret in the gray light.

Farina sighed, crossed her arms warding off a chilly wind, and waited. Hearing coyotes and bobcats, owls in the tree on the north side of the house, she tapped her heel on the stoop, and flung her arms to her side, giving up going inside.

The door shut. The light in the house extinguished. The moon rose higher catching the wings of bats flying from tree to tree, and an opossum waddled into the field.

Like Christmas luminaries, the field brightened. A long stream of small lights snaked their way from the horizon through the fields to the house.

Farina's cell phone rang, and Razzy only said, "Look outside." Farina lifted the curtain from the window.

Out of the house letting the moonlight afford her safe journey over the grass, Farina stood a safe distance from the strange balls.

The Lady in the Ladybug

Razzy swept his hand over the globes, and they gathered into one bright light. He glanced over to Farina and said, "Go inside and get a blanket."

She dutifully obliged and returned with the blanket off the couch. She handed to him the red nubby Navajo blanket, not asking what he needed the covering for, and finding her answer while watching him throw the cover over the globes and scoop them up and over onto the front seat of the pickup.

Razzy sat on the driver's seat and waited for Farina. She pulled herself up into the cab, sitting as close to the door as possible, avoiding the blanket. Farina glanced at him, wondering why he kept so silent and solemn while he traveled Marquez Road to the rocked road, and to the highway.

"When the asteroid exploded way back, these globes of light fell to earth," Razzy recited.

"They're an alien life form?"

Slowing the pickup and pulling off to the shoulder, he reached under the blanket, and showed one of the globes to her.

She rolled it over the palm of her hands, curiously studying the flecks of silver. There were no masses for a brain or eyes or any openings in the clear globe.

"The silver flecks power the light."

She placed it back under the blanket, wiping her hands on her clothing.

"They must have intelligence, how else do they function?"

"Don't think we can send one off for study, do you?"

Farina agreed. "No."

"My great-great grandfather used them for gathering crops in the dark. He also found they heal."

The headlights of the pickup illuminated the H on the blue sign on the highway. The arrow pointed north.

She squinted at Razzy when he stopped closest to the front door of the hospital. He hopped out, beckoning her. "C'mon."

The Lady in the Ladybug

He mopped the blanket over the globes and held them close to his chest.

She stared at him holding the pickup door open for her, he meaning for her to crawl across the front seat. Scooting over it, she shut the door, and walked behind Razzy taking long determined steps to the hospital. She looked at the time. It was ten till eight.

The smell of disinfectant fell upon them once inside and a faint odor of the nurses' perfume drifted down the hallway. They noticed her and Razzy going into room number six, looking up from the laptops they typed.

Sugar lay unconscious, oxygen tubing around her nose, IV bags dripping into veins. Razzy nodded his head toward the door. Farina closed it and pulled the window shades.

Razzy laid the blanket on her chest, and pulled it loose, letting the globes roll over her and onto the mattress. The lights rolled to a stop in the folds of bed coverings and brightened the entire room.

Razzy examined his mother's tightly closed eyes like she were in pain. He had no idea how long to keep the globes near her, on her, around her. The warmth of the lights drew perspiration, and beads bubbled on Sugar's forehead, and on the puffiness around her eyes. The room kept bright and warm until the globes extinguished. They looked useless, like rubber balls that didn't bounce.

In the faint light of morning, from a painful expression to one of waking up, Sugar popped her eyes open. "Where am I?"

Razzy quickly gathered the globes inside the blanket, and then he pressed the call button.

"May I help you?"

"My mother is awake."

"We'll be right there."

"How do you feel, mother?"

She blinked her eyes and squinted. The nurse hurried into the room.

"How?" Sugar cleared her throat, "How long have I been in this room?"

"Just a few hours," the nurse answered. "Just don't worry about anything." The nurse assured her with a touch on her shoulder. "We will call Doctor Marquit to update your progress."

"I'm starving."

Razzy and Farina chuckled.

"Do you hurt anywhere?"

"My hip hurts. But why did that man have my shining cloths? Who released those grasshoppers on my farm?"

"I wouldn't worry about that now," Razzy said, looking at the time and kissing his mother. They said their goodbyes and exited the room, leaving the nurse tending to Sugar.

"Can I have a shower?"

"I'll send the aide in."

Sugar reached for the telephone and pressed numbers. "Atla, I'm awake. What's going on at the store? On the local news? Over and over? Oh no…"

An aide walked into the room pushing a wheel chair.

"I'll call you back, Atla."

The aide wheeled Sugar to the shower, opened the door for her and turned on the water, letting it warm. "Call when you are finished."

She returned to the room to take off the bedding. After the bedspread went into a plastic bag, a rubber ball rolled across the floor. She caught it and held it up, trying to discover why the specks of silver lighted like weak streaks of lightning. Placing it on the counter beside the sink, the aide walked out of the room, went to a laptop and typed. Sugar's nurse typed on a laptop, charting her progress.

The shower call light bell sounded. The aide scurried down the hallway. She opened the shower door, "Are you ready?"

"Yes, that felt so good."

"A much needed shower does lift spirits, doesn't it?"

"Four- three- two- one." Chubb pointed at Sugar. "Pumpkins fresh from the garden for autumn desserts with flavored coffee are by far the most tempting thing besides chocolate on Halloween. Lonny and Bolynne have created their original recipe for pumpkin layered pie with a chocolate drizzle."

Sugar walked out of view of the camera, rubbing her hip, while Lonny and Bolynne went on with the show. Customers walked past with shopping carts piled high with fruits and vegetables.

"Hello, how are you today?" Sugar asked.

The woman in a jogging suit smiled and replied, "Great, thank you."

"Hello, Mrs. Hart, you look great today."

"I feel great."

Sugar picked up an apple that rolled off the display, and hit a pumpkin. Pumpkins lined the store from one end to the other. The fairytale plump round pumpkins were popular, but the larger ones were the best for carving and adding a candle for a spooky jack o lantern.

Television sets installed around the store showed the recorded segment of Lonny and Bolynne on the farm. Bobby and Razzy cut pumpkins off the vine. They loaded them into trucks to bring to the store. Bobby carved a jack o lantern, explaining each step.

A few customers watched. "I think he's had some experience carving a pumpkin."

Sugar smiled and watched Bobby poking out the eyes in the jack o lantern face, nose, and teeth. The only problem it was day. Can't show a glowing pumpkin then. Bobby proudly displayed the pumpkin on the stacked straw bales, and in the background came Chicken Soup across the harvested field. Razzy took notice, signaling Chubb to stop filming.

The Lady in the Ladybug

Sugar heard laughter across the store. "Big chicken! Wow! Things do grow large on that farm."

Sugar giggled and went to the television set. Chubb counted down.

"Sugar, come taste our pumpkin cream pie," Bolynne said, presenting the dessert to her.

Sugar scooped up a heaping amount and lapped it down, grinning ear to ear. "Mmm, so good, Bolynne, you and Lonny have a great recipe. Shall we pass slices to the shoppers?"

"Yes, we shall," Lonny said, pulling the serving cart out behind the counter filled with plates of the pie.

Ten customers reached for a plate and Chubb followed the crowd for fifteen seconds, and then he turned the camera on Sugar.

"Our first pumpkin carving contest is coming up," she said, holding a jack o lantern. "The rules are on the show's website, seen here on the screen. Purchase a pumpkin from either of my two stores, and carve your best face. Bring the pumpkin to either store on October thirtieth at four thirty for judging. We provide the lighting for each pumpkin. Bring us your best and we'll do the rest." She paused for a breath of air. "The judges will choose two winners from each store. Come in costume for another great prize, and enjoy a magic show while you wait for the judges final decisions. The winners will be featured on Sugar Martin's Cooking Show."

Lonny pushed in front of the camera showing a freshly baked pie. "Another prize is a pumpkin pie baked by me and Bolynne. It's just not another plain pumpkin pie anymore, we add surprises!"

Sugar and Bolynne chuckled. "Next week," Bolynne said, "It is more Indian Summer recipes from our kitchen." Bolynne waved goodbye into the camera, and slowly made her way through the shoppers with more plates of dessert. Chubb followed Sugar shaking hands with customers, commenting on their purchases, asking what they were baking, or eating at tonight's dinner. Sugar laughed and joked, having a good time.

122

Bolynne and Lonny talked with some customers, giving autographs and hugs, hearing praises from viewers.

Hugh snuck through the shoppers, snuggling up to Sugar. She smiled and introduced him.

"This is my husband, Hugh Martin."

"Hello, hello."

Lonny and Bolynne turned their heads when they heard her introduce him.

"Sugar, you are going home, aren't you?" Hugh asked.

"Yes, I'm going to put my feet up," she said, anticipating his next comment.

"May I drive you?" he asked.

"Well, sure," she took his arm, "If you're going that way."

"I am." He grinned leading her to the front door.

Sugar waved goodbye.

"After you," Hugh said.

Sugar smiled and kept eyeing his face for a genuine smile. He seemed to be happy. Many times she had doubted he really loved her. Maybe it was infatuation. Maybe it was her wrestling costume that he fell in love with way back, twenty-six years ago. Well, whatever he felt, he was in love for twenty-one of those years. Now, he's in love again?

They walked out of the store into the parking lot. It was flooded with vehicles from all over the United States. RVs, trailers, and vans packed to the brim competing for a parking spot. Hugh pointed at the low-slung red car with the top down. The back seat had a few white feathers stuck in the fabric. She looked the other direction, trying not to bring too much attention to it.

Zipping out of the parking lot onto the street, Sugar noticed the billboard for Three apartments.

"Uh."

"What?"

"Anyone heard from Lee Three?"

"He got what he deserved. Those USDA agents questioned him and he admitted he took your cloths. Found out he had ordered two truckloads of grasshoppers. That must have cost money. But he did it and not sure if he was in this alone, or had help."

"Help? Like who?"

"I heard a name, Reva Little. Farina admitted she knew her, worked with her at the state building."

Hugh stopped at the light, and handed to her an eight by ten picture of a huge home on a lake.

"That's yours, Sugar. It's all yours, whenever you want to retire, or, get away."

"Hugh, where is it?"

"On the back is the address and directions."

"It's ..." she looked at the back of the glossy.

"You like it?"

"Beautiful."

The light turned green. They passed restaurants sporting their organic food, businesses with all organic ingredients in food, clothing, and ink. Water purifying systems were as common as soda pop machines.

"It's all yours."

Sugar looked down, letting the picture slip to the side, "Do you really think I would live in this house?"

He glanced at her. "Well, why not?" He stared at her for an answer.

"I can't leave the farm. I've got my chickens and garden, and stores, and a wintertime job."

Hugh stopped at an intersection. "Razzy told me I should grow up and settle down."

Sugar stretched her neck and leaned forward to him to say, "And are you?"

The Lady in the Ladybug

Halloween

A little girl dropped coins onto the checkout counter at Sugar Martin's Organic Store 1. The clerk counted, smiling; sympathetic she didn't have enough money to purchase the five dollar pumpkin, she reached into her trouser pocket and contributed three dollars.

"Thank you," she said, sweetly.

Sugar smiled at her clerk. "Do that much?"

"Once in a while," she said.

"Well, that's wonderful you helped out, but let the manager know instead, we'll help," she said, winking. Sugar noticed the orange banner with black lettering above the pumpkin 'patch.' The paint had dripped down from the letters, causing it to look like font used for a horror movie.

Ghost pumpkins, gold pumpkins, and leck pumpkins set in a bed of shimmering streamers on a green shag carpet. A poster cut out of Lonny and Bolynne stood behind it, and a poster stating two winners from each store will appear on Sugar Martin's Cooking Show with their carved pumpkins. In addition, a pumpkin pie baked by the very hands of Lonny and Bolynne.

Girls chattered about that while they chose their fairytale pumpkins. "I'm carving my pumpkin like the face of a mouse."

One blurted out. "I'm carving mine scary."

Sugar heard a group of junior high students thundering into the store, heading toward the pumpkins.

They giggled and laughed, choosing their pumpkins, teasing each other with them, almost dropping them, and running to the check out. Boys stood by Bolynne's cardboard cutout and stared into her face.

"Bolynne's hot," one of the boys said, joining the girls.

The students pulled out big bills to pay for the five dollar pumpkins.

The Lady in the Ladybug

Bobby sipped a brew of orange cappuccino coffee, handing a list to Sugar. She looked it over, "The lights are at the farm, Bobby. We ordered solar balls to put in all the pumpkins. They'll be charging in the sunshine."

Bobby scribbled that on his list.

"Oh," Sugar added, "Don't pick them up until the night of the judging."

"Will do, Sugar."

"How are you feeling, Bobby? Your liver problems on the mend?" she asked.

"I feel better. I'm eating healthy, all organics, of course."

"Have you seen Lee Three?"

"I haven't been in that store since the night of the tree festival."

"Really? Is it still open?"

"I don't know."

"Let's drive over there."

"Why not?" Bobby said, pulling his keys out of his trouser pocket.

Sugar followed Bobby out the door and to his pickup. He opened the door for her, and she pulled herself in it, noticing the cleanliness. He turned onto Turnage Street, waited for several vans and pulled into traffic. He turned south and traveled five blocks. They turned into the parking lot. Bobby looked for Three's pickup. It wasn't there.

Bobby watched the busy front door and looked at the time, nearing noon. "Three goes to lunch at noon exactly," he said, slowing to a stop.

"How did you get involved with Three in the beginning? My cousins said there was a newspaper article about you."

Bobby turned off the pickup.

"I met Reva Little in San Amez last year. We dated. She wanted to get rich. Had all these schemes. Then she realized what could happen in Glassburgh. She asked me to help her. The only thing I had to do was say I was healthier eating the produce, and work at a store to

126

help promote the food. I didn't know she was trying to scam people. But eating healthy does make you a better person. I know it." Bobby opened the pickup door.

"You aren't going in, are you?"

"I'm going to march right in and ask where Lee Three is and put your mind at ease. Be back in a flash."

Sugar watched him go to the front door. She pulled her hat down around her face, trying to avoid any curious onlookers, but watched the busy parking lot. She recognized her customers going into the store.

Wonder what they are buying in there? There was Atla's cousin coming out with three or four sacks. "Uh, Dr. Marquit?" Many people she knew were shopping. Disgusted, she quit watching. What in the world were they buying in there? She looked back. Mrs. Bandstra? "Okay, that's it." She opened the pickup door, limped across the parking lot, and flagged her down.

"Hello, Mrs. Bandstra."

"Sugar!"

"Shocked to see me here?" Sugar slyly looked at the food in her sacks. "A sale going on?"

"Don't you like to save money?"

"Uh… oh, excuse me." She abandoned Mrs. Bandstra for Bobby departing the store, and returning to the pickup.

"They said he's on vacation."

"And I hope that's a long ways away from here."

Will You Marry Me?

Chicken Soup looked up from nibbling the grass when she heard a rumble on Marquez Road. She sniffed the air, and stepped forward to smell the person erupting from the tin can.

The Lady in the Ladybug

"Hey, Chicken Soup, don't eat me today, I come with good news." Chris petted Chicken Soup's beak and swayed around her legs to the front door. Chicken Soup followed and stood behind him as he knocked. Sugar opened the door, and smiled at Chris and squinted at Chicken Soup peering in the house.

"No, the chicken can't come in, but you can, Chris."

"Thanks, a check, my dear."

Sugar's eyes grew wider. "One hundred dollars? From what?"

"Advertising money from the show. That's your share."

"Lonny and Bolynne were given a check, I hope?"

"Yes, same amount."

"Each?" She asked holding the check at arm's length.

"Yes," he chuckled.

"Good, they need all the money possible. College, you know." She tucked the check into her pocket.

"That's not the entire reason I'm here, the cooking show was picked up in Albuquerque."

"That's wonderful."

"Advertising dollars will double, triple!"

"I hope so," she said, crossing her fingers.

"Another reason I'm here, we need thirteen pumpkins for the haunted house."

"We're picking all the remaining pumpkins today. I'll drop them off."

Hugh marched into the kitchen from the back door. "Hello!" he called out to Chris.

"Hey, Mr. Martin."

"Call me Hugh," he said, opening the fridge and screwing open a bottle of iced cappuccino. "We have plenty." Hugh held up the bottle.

"Sure."

Hugh took another bottle and met Chris halfway into the living room.

The Lady in the Ladybug

"That reminds me, Chris, what about my own line of water?" Sugar asked.

"Not a bad idea," he said. "I'll look into it. Thanks for the cappuccino."

"Goodbye, Chris," Sugar said, following him out.

Chicken Soup ran across the road to her thicket near the garage. A semi slowly made its way to the barn.

"Good the mites and aphids are here," Sugar said.

"What?" Chris asked, lips curled.

"We order a winter's supply of food for the ladybugs. They're aggressive predators when it comes to eating."

"Really." Chris took another gulp of cappuccino, finishing it before sitting in the convertible, and perplexed where to dispose the bottle.

"I'll recycle the bottle, Chris." She took it from him, slipped it into her dress pocket, and waved goodbye.

Razzy honked at Chris whizzing past, meeting a UPS van.

Hugh came out of the house, stopped in front of Sugar, and looking into her eyes, he kissed her.

Shocked, Sugar touched her lips. Hugh turned back and smiled while going to the barn. The UPS driver honked and slid to a stop in the driveway. He ran out with a large package. Sugar signed her name and thanked him, reading the labels. She carried the large box inside and set it on the table, cutting the mailing tape with a kitchen knife, reaching down through the packing peanuts for the instructions. "Pull the red tab out of the slot on the bottom of each light. Set them in the sun two days before use."

She scooped out the peanuts, tossing them into the trash. Out the door with the box she traipsed, tugged the little tabs out, setting each globe on the lawn in the bright sunshine by the front door. Two hundred clear golf ball size solar globes— she hoped that would be enough for the pumpkin-carving contest.

The Lady in the Ladybug

Razzy and Hugh came out of the barn, laughing, slapping each other on the back. Sugar crooked her neck, raised one eyebrow, and watched them walk to the back door. She heard the old rusty barbecue grill roll out of the little shed on the other side of the house. Paper-thin metal on the bottom couldn't hold much more weight; probably the briquettes would fall right through. Around the corner of the house she trotted to add her womanly advice.

"That rusty old— where'd they go?" Suction from the front door opening shut the back door. She plopped her fists on her hips, "Now what are they up to?" She walked into the kitchen, and stopped. She stared at the table. Slowly, with eyes tearing, she reached out to the small card on the dozen red roses.

Sugar, please be my special guest tonight here on the farm for a barbecue at six o'clock sharp.

Hugh.

"Hmmm. A guest in my own house?"

She really didn't want to put on one of her polka dot or striped dresses she wore every day. She wanted something special, something modern. So, it was shopping, and she grabbed her purse and headed to the garage. "Camel Sue's, here I come!" she yelled, walking quickly to the garage.

She backed the low-slung car out, kicking up a few pebbles on her way out of the driveway. Checking the rearview mirrors, there were no chickens, no ladybugs— just a sunshiny autumn day — no farming and no working — only a day for playing.

At the corner of Marquez Road and the highway, she turned north, headed to Savoy and looked out over her farmland stretching to the sky. On and on forever it went with miles and miles of harvested ground basking in the warmth of angled rays of the autumn sun.

The Lady in the Ladybug

She reached Savoy, and pushed into traffic and weaved into the lanes she needed. In Glassburgh, seeing the sign for Camel Sue's high in the sky, it competed for recognition from other specialty shops surrounding that industrious block.

Expensive cars lined the streets and parking lots. She snuggled her classic auto into a parking space and crawled out. Camel Sue's door opened automatically and the purified air of the store enveloped every human sense. The fashionable clerks smiled, asking if she were looking for anything special.

"Yes, I am, a casual at home special dress that doesn't make me look like it's for a special occasion."

"I see. Let's try the Colangelo line of dresses. Follow me."

She led her to a rack of dresses of the colors of the rainbow. A robin's egg blue sundress with a lace shawl brought out a smile. "Perfect!"

"The changing room is to your left."

The clerk carried it for her to the changing room. The door opened and Farina exited with two dresses over her arm.

"Sugar."

"Hello, Farina."

"That's a beautiful color of blue, what's the occasion?"

"Tonight."

"Really? The barbecue?" She beamed.

"Yes—"

"Well, I'll see you there." Smiling, Sugar entered the dressing room.

❂

Sugar fluffed her hair, pushed in a bobby pin, and rolled on lipstick. Hearing Hugh and Razzy fumbling around in the kitchen, she stepped into her shoes and made an entrance. Razzy took a double look at her. Hugh turned around.

"You're—gorgeous—Sugar."

"Well, thank you. You two look dashing in white shirts."

Farina came in from outside with a small sack, her mouth grew wider in awe of Sugar. "How stunning!"

"Thank you." Hearing the Bossa Nova coming from the CD player, she smiled at Hugh, remembering.

"You ladies sit at the table outside with your glasses of wine, and we'll bring out the chow," Hugh said.

"Smells really good," Farina said.

Sugar agreed, heading outdoors to card tables covered with plastic. Chilled wine and wine glasses awaited them. A platter of steaks, potatoes, and corn came out on a cart that Hugh pushed. He served Sugar; Razzy served Farina. In a glow of the orange and red sunset, Razzy held his wine cup high. "To the most beautiful women in the world."

"Here here," Hugh said.

Farina dabbed her mouth with a napkin.

"May I have this dance?" Razzy asked.

She stood, taking his hand.

Hugh held out his hand to Sugar. She placed her hand on his shoulder, and looked down at her feet, trying to step in time to the Bossa Nova. "Just like we learned in Brazil, Sugar."

"Oh, that was a long time ago, Hugh."

Razzy took Farina's hand, and pulled her next to him, and their arms entwined around one another.

They slowly moved to the music, saying sweet things. He stepped back from her and waved one hand into the sky. They turned to watch the unfolding display across the horizon. The globes of lights spread out

w i l l y o u m a r r y m e?

Farina gasped. "Yes!" Razzy hugged her, who watched him wave his hand over the horizon once more. Farina dried her cheeks, watching the dimming lights reappear

w i l l y o u m a r r y m e a g a i n?

They turned to Sugar and Hugh. Sugar's lips parted and stared at the horizon.

Magic Show

Bobby bounced over the highway near the harvested corn field, catching glimpses of light near the horizon behind Sugar's house. He slowed to a stop and squinted, "Who in the world would be asking me to get married?" He turned on the dirt road, and stopped. Taking a box out of the pickup, he stepped over the freshly churned earth and grabbed one solar light. It was warm and had the strangest texture to it. "Weird." He picked up the requested two hundred, placing them in a box.

"Sugar sure made it difficult," he said, grumbling.

Costumed children presented their jack o lanterns to Lonny and Bolynne inside Sugar Martin's Organic Store 1 on the glassless side. Children waited in line at the newly installed coffee counter giggling, laughing, whining, and stating their name and telephone number to them.

"Can you see that my pumpkin's face looks like the wicked witch in the Wizard of Oz?" A little witch asked.

"Oh, it does," Bolynne said, tagging it.

Frankenstein plopped on the counter his grinning jack o lantern with a scarred cheek.

"I'm Antony Callais."

"Hello, Antony," Lonny said, writing down his name, asking the spelling. Behind Antony were vampires, fairies, and a witch doctor admitting their jack o lanterns for judging. The last goblin handed over her pumpkin in protest.

"You'll get it back, sweetie," Bolynne said. She frowned at Bolynne the entire time she tagged the last pumpkin.

"Goblins!" Lonny said, loudly, "Take your jack o lantern outside and set them down outside in front of the building." He pointed toward the front of the store, and led the way.

Bolynne scrolled the screen of her cell phone, "Atla, one hundred thirty pumpkins."

Lonny pointed to where he wanted the jack o lanterns lined up at. He walked backward and beckoned them down further to the end of the building.

"Good, goblins, thanks," Lonny said.

Many witches and fairies forfeited their jack o lanterns to witch Atla at the television set in store 2. Her dark eyebrows scrutinized each entrant. "Hello, little goblin, you look really good in that costume." A little witch teetered on her high heels, waiting for her turn. "Wow, good makeup."

"Thank you."

Atla watched slobbering vampires waiting behind princesses and cheerleaders. Farther away football players, hippies, and a werewolf poked the tomatoes. Swashbucklers and pirates dueled with cucumbers until mothers intervened. A black cat chased a mouse around the check stand.

A little ladybug walked in holding hands with a ballerina. Sugar's eyes brightened in glee over the costumes. She said hello to the father carrying the pumpkins for them. She pointed them toward the big witch who entered pumpkins into the judging.

The Lady in the Ladybug

Sugar watched Atla tag those two entrants, checking the time. She had entered eighty-three. She flipped up her black gown, retrieved her cell phone out of her shirt pocket. "Bobby, we have a total of two hundred and thirteen pumpkins. Best hunt up some more lights. Candles if you have to."

"Got it covered, Atla," he answered.

Sugar picked up the intercom phone. "Goblins! Please carry your jack o lantern outside for judging."

A flurry of goblins appeared, and followed Sugar out the front door.

Atla took notice of some of the more careless goblins running with a jack o lantern, bumping into others. "Careful!" She called out. With all the jack o lanterns on their way out the door, she followed them outside. The entrants set their pumpkin down close to the building.

The speaker crackled on. "Magic Show! Magic Show! Come watch the magician perform dazzling acts. You won't believe your eyes!" Sugar announced. Children ran inside excitedly chattering about the tricks they might see.

Silas and Appalonia erupted from their pickup and took instructions from Witch Atla. She handed to them a notebook and two pencils. Bobby set the box of globes down, "Perfect," Atla remarked, picking one up, and instantly dropping it. "What are these?"

"Solar globes," Bobby said.

"They feel like eyeballs."

Bobby parked by the pumpkins nestled against the building on store 1. He set the box on the cement and put a globe into each pumpkin. Their faces came to life one by one, frowning or grinning, all seemed to be happy with a light inside them.

"Magic show! Magic show! Come watch a magician perform dazzling acts. You won't believe your eyes!" Bolynne announced to the children waiting for the judges' decision. Goblins ran into the store to the coffee shop.

The Lady in the Ladybug

A man in a swallowtail coat took his top hat off and produced a rabbit. "Let me introduce myself, I am Mark the Magnificent, displaying magic for your pleasure on this very special event. My twin brother, Clark the Marvelous, is at Sugar's other store across town, performing the same acts as I. You will be fascinated!"

A little soldier boy pushed his way to the front of the crowd, desperately trying to see the tricks. "I can't see. I wanna see!"

Hands grabbed him and plopped him on a pair of muscular shoulders. The boy looked down at Lonny's face. "Thanks."

"No problem."

Mrs. Bandstra held onto Chris Tatro's arm and walked past the magic show on their way outside to judge the jack o lanterns.

The magician asked for a volunteer.

"Me. Me. Me."

"I need someone bigger—" He scanned the crowd and nodded. "You."

Bolynne grinned. "Me?" She smiled, a little hesitant but stood on the spot he indicated and watched him slowly swing a pocket watch in front of her face, until her eyes closed. She slowly tipped backward, her feet raised up off the floor.

"Ahh!" the children said.

He suspended Bolynne in air horizontally. He raised her higher and lower, showing there were no wires or strings attached. The audience applauded and then Mark the Magnificent reversed the process.

Bolynne landed on her feet. He snapped his fingers and she gasped awake. Chris and Mrs. Bandstra interrupted more applause by waving a piece of paper in the air above the children.

"Do we have winners?" Lonny asked.

"Yes."

"And the winners are!" Chris said. "Twenty-two."

Raggedy Ann jumped up and down. "I won, I won!"

"Eighty-four."

The Lady in the Ladybug

"Yippee!" A scarecrow yelled.

"Congratulations! Twenty-two and eighty-four come up for a picture." Chris motioned them to the counter. Bolynne brought out two pumpkin pies. "Say cheese!"

"We'll call you for your appearance on the cooking show," Lonny said.

"I can't wait," Raggedy Ann said.

Atla floated above the floor. Clark the Marvelous waved his wand under her and over her. "No strings. No wires. All magic!"

"Wow!" The children echoed.

Sugar watched with her mouth wide open. She bent over Atla, seeming to be asleep. "Atla," she whispered.

"Shh-shh!" Clark the Marvelous said.

Silas and Appalonia glanced at each other. Silas winked. Appalonia shook her head unbelieving, and handed the paper with two numbers scrawled in red ink to Sugar.

Clark the Marvelous waved his palms toward Atla, and raised her up into the air and above the children. She floated over them, her black hair draping down like a wet mop. The children looked up with open mouths, and watched entranced as he motioned her back to the starting point and commanded her to her feet. The children erupted applause. Atla opened her eyes and fluttered her eyelashes trying to focus.

Sugar applauded the loudest, grinning. She stood by the magician, waving the papers, and read the winning numbers to the anxious entrants. "Thirteen, Maya Chavez! Thirty-one, Michael Pool!"

Squeals echoed through the group of children. The werewolf and ladybug struggled free from the group to stand beside Sugar.

"Hello, little ladybug. Congratulations." Sugar held her hand, while putting her other hand on the werewolf's shoulder.

"Say cheese!" Appalonia said. The camera flashed on the grinning werewolf and smiling ladybug.

The Lady in the Ladybug

Silas presented the winners with one pumpkin pie each. "Sugar will contact you later about the dates of your cooking show appearance," Appalonia said.

"Thank you," the ladybug said.

"Thanks," said the werewolf, joining a group of friends passing by.

"Yes, thank you," said the ladybug's father, taking the pie.

"You're Mr. Chavez?" Sugar asked.

"Yes."

"Where did you get the idea to be a ladybug?"

"Playing on one in the park," she said, almost whispering.

Sugar's eyebrows rose, remembering a mother and child there once while Cleopatra waited for her.

"Let's go," Mr. Chavez said, letting Maya take the lead.

Sugar grinned, waving goodbye.

Atla hung pictures of the winning jack o lanterns below the office windows.

"Wasn't she adorable?" Sugar asked her, watching them depart the store.

The little ladybug held onto her winning jack o lantern and climbed into her father's white Envoy.

He proceeded out of the parking lot, waiting for cars leaving the store, and entrants taking their lighted jack o lanterns with them as they ran or walked home. The Envoy went three blocks and stopped.

The porch light revealed the many other jack o lanterns on steps and bales of hay. Maya ran to the door, carefully holding onto her prize cat face jack o lantern so realistically carved, the eyes danced with the rolling globe of light inside. She punched in the code on the keyless entry and went straight to her mother lying on the couch.

"Look, Mommy, I won."

"You did?"

"Yep, she also won this pumpkin pie," Mr. Chavez said.

"I'm going to be on the cooking show."

The Lady in the Ladybug

"Wow."

"Here, Mommy, hold the pumpkin."

"Picture time," Mr. Chavez said.

Mrs. Chavez tugged down the pink scarf on her head.

"Say—statistics—good one!"

"Off to bed, Miss Ladybug, school tomorrow."

"Good night, sweetheart," Mrs. Chavez said.

"Night, I love you," Maya said.

"Same here."

She blew her mother a kiss on the way to the bedroom.

Mr. Chavez sat beside her, took her hand, and kissed it. "I'm beat, coming to bed?"

"Soon."

He reached over, kissed her cheek, and left the room. She smiled and looked down into the pumpkin, ready to blow out the light, instead she pulled out a round globe, noticing silver strands floating inside.

She turned it over and over, watching slivers of silver swim through the fluid, almost as if they were a living thing, not strips of metal. She felt her forehead, dabbing away the perspiration droplets, seeming worried, but rather her demeanor changed from struggling to peaceful.

With the globe returned into the pumpkin, she set it on the stand near the window, and with new energy, she went to the bedroom, smiling.

⬡

Sugar departed the front door carrying a morning cup of coffee, and looking over at the red and yellow leaves on the few trees around the barn and garage. Amazed the brilliant yellow and deep red leaves had stayed on for so long. She took in a deep breath, smelling the crisp air, wondering when the first snow would arrive. She took a few more careful barefoot steps outside. She laid her eyes on the grass. Frowning, she pulled her cell phone out of her pocket.

"Bobby, you didn't use the solar lights for the pumpkins?"

"Yeah, I did."

"They're here in the yard," she said, picking one up.

"I got them out of a field, they spelled out will you marry me."

"Oh, no." Sugar closed her eyes. "We let loose the healing globes into Glassburgh."

"Is that bad?"

"No, I guess not."

End of the Season

Sugar had a spring to her step on the way to the front door. On it, she posted, closing in two weeks, *thank you for your patronage, see you in the summer.*

With harvest over, the shelves were almost bare. A late crop of zucchini and tomatoes, beans, and cucumbers along with squash, beets, and lettuce, were all that remained.

A flurry of customers swarmed over the produce, grabbing, pushing one another out of the way, and arguing over the last few beets.

"Mrs. Chavez was cured of cancer, why wasn't I? She shops here, I've seen her."

Sugar stopped, listened. She remembered seeing a young woman with a pink hat on with a little girl at the park. Rosa said her niece was only 30, and had breast cancer. That was Maya's mother.

Sugar went to the office and sat. She didn't know what to do. What had she done? What had Lee Three done to this town? Won't everyone blame her? What if she had cancer, wouldn't she want cured? Why would Lee Three say such a thing about the produce in Sands County? It was a lie.

But she had a cure. She cured Silas. Wouldn't she help herself? Razzy? Her own family? Share this miracle with the world? The whole world would be at her doorstep.

Sugar laid her head on the desk and sobbed.

Jo walked into Director Welch's office. He gestured at a chair. She sat, spreading out papers.

"Something unusual is going on in Glassburgh," she said.

Welch crossed his arms, warily eyeing her. "There's always something unusual in that town."

"A woman has been miraculously cured of breast cancer. She's not the only one. Several people in Glassburgh are cancer free, disease free, and all happened in the past six months."

"And you think it's the food?" He smirked.

"Something is doing it."

"How many people?" he asked.

"At last count, fifty-three. Diabetes gone, tumors gone, emphysema cured, and just last week, the cancer patients in Savoy on the edge of Glassburgh, all reported their cancers—gone."

"I need more proof."

"I'll try to find it. Wouldn't it be wonder—"

"The whole world will be in Sands County." Welch tapped his ink pen on the desk.

Jo slightly nodded, looking down, understanding the devastation it could bring.

Welch cleared his throat. Jo gathered her papers and departed.

The Lady in the Ladybug

One Year Later

A fast muscle car zigzagged through the parking lot of Sugar Martin's Organic Food Store. Dix Caddo and Monterey Montoya exited the convertible and walked arm in arm to the front door. Monterey laughed, clipping inside the store, and stopped abruptly at seeing the large tomatoes, beets, broccoli, and carrots.

"You weren't exaggerating, Dix," she said.

"Would I lie to you?"

"Then, everything must be true."

"See for yourself," he said, sweeping his arm to the right.

Sugar stood with her hands on her hips. She noted Monterey looking her up and down at her knee length blue and white polka dot dress and large rubber boots ripped at the toes.

"Welcome to my store, Monterey, so glad you could come to Glassburgh. Come to the farm later, there's a lot more there to see."

Monterey smiled. "So I've heard."

The End

The Lady in the Ladybug

Sharona Black lives in Smith Center, Kansas, center of the United States, and home of Home on the Range. She spent twenty years in the grocery business, which was an inspiration for this novel, The Lady in the Ladybug.

Stories published:

Deeply Rooted Hadrosaur Tales 8
Fur Midnight Carnival Vol 1. No. 4
Valley of the Indus Women Shadowland summer issue 2003
Moffit Maley A Big Book of Strange Weird & Wonderful 2
Put Like This Mystic Signals Issue 19 August 2013

Scripts

Home on the Range Lone Chimney Films

Books

The Little Tornado self-published

Awards

The Little Tornado Kansas Voices 2008 second place for prose
Spring Giggled Heartland Herald-Echo poetry contest

Made in the USA
Charleston, SC
07 August 2015